RAVENS HOLLOW

Printed in Australia
Cover design by Shawline Publishing Group Pty Ltd
Images in this book are copyright approved for Shawline Publishing Group Pty Ltd
Illustrations within this book are copyright approved for Shawline Publishing Group Pty Ltd

First Printing: February 2023
Shawline Publishing Group Pty Ltd
www.shawlinepublishing.com.au

Paperback ISBN 978-1-9228-5103-1
eBook ISBN 978-1-9228-5104-8

Distributed by Shawline Distribution and Lightningsource Global

A catalogue record for this work is available from the National Library of Australia

More great Shawline titles can be found here:

New titles also available through Books@Home Pty Ltd.
Subscribe today - www.booksathome.com.au

RAVENS HOLLOW

JUDITH ROOK

For Lindsay Gordon Rook 1919-2002

A special thank you to Jan Dunwoodie and Georgia Hempel
with appreciation for the help, encouragement and support
bringing the work together. And Bradley Shaw for instigating
the publishing of this fictional story.

THE SENTINELS

We are the soul of Ravens Hollow.
We have been reborn again and again
To serve and oversee this land
That we claim as our own.
We are the custodians,
With our black armour and golden eyes.
Our arm is as strong as steel.
With vigilance we defend.
As we fly, we guard all we survey.
We are the Judge and Jury.
We dispatch,
We execute,
We rectify,
We are here to right the wrong.
We are a brotherhood,
The Sentinels that stand strong,
To protect and save our given world.

Judith Rook

1

LEE PING

The stench of excrement and mud was only relieved by the slight whispering breeze sweeping across the giant eucalypts that surrounded the camp, leaving their sweet perfume lingering in the air. The trees were one of the few things Lee Ping could look at with any positivity in this journey he found himself embarking on.

Australia was a word Lee Ping had never heard. Everyone was full of talk about this country where gold had been found. This country was said to be on the other side of the world, many miles away, had gold in the rivers and in the ground, just for the taking.

The company Lee Ping had worked for since he was old enough to do so, as his father had done before him, was sending him to this far off land.

He had no choice. He was promised great wealth and that Mu, his wife of one year and his week-old son, Tay, would be paid a percentage of his wage every week. They would be looked after while he was away. As an obedient servant to the company, his country and his family, Lee must do his duty. Along with many of his countrymen, Lee Ping set sail for Australia.

Behind his brave face, Lee Ping's heart was breaking. He wanted to scream out that he didn't want to go. He would miss his loved family and his country, his home. Nowhere else on earth could mean as much to him.

As always, he would be obedient and try to bring wealth and pride to Mu and Tay's future, giving them a firm foundation. That was what Lee Ping had to believe, otherwise he would not have been able to go on.

Bravely he accepted his fate. But nothing would have prepared him for the journey and the conditions they all would have to endure.

After a year in this unforgiving land, he had almost given up hope of ever seeing Mu's sweet smile or feeling the softness of his son's skin again. He had worked hard every day. He tried to believe he would be wealthy, but he knew it was all a dream. The company would be the richer for all his hard work.

He was so tired by the end of the day it was all he could do to find his tent and crawl into his blanket on the hard ground. The days seemed so long and the nights so short. The seasons were extreme. His skin burned and blistered as the sun scorched his body. It was a fight to find and store good drinking water, but when the rain and cold came it was hard to plough through the mud. Some days, it was so deep his tired legs hardly had the strength to get through the morass to his tent. His hands were purple and his bones ached. It was hard to find dry wood for the fire. Some nights, Lee Ping wept until he fell asleep.

He had been lucky he had not come down with any of the many illnesses that spread through the camps. He was losing condition and heart, but was doing his best not to disgrace his family or country.

On good days, he would go to The Golden Nugget, the only hotel in the high street where you could get food and drink and other recreational goods the body may need. Sometimes he would share a pipe with his fellow countrymen, but that only made him more homesick than ever. So, he didn't indulge too often.

He needed new shoes and some warmer clothes, so he saved as much of his wages as he could. There was so much gold to be found and people were getting very rich, but not the ones loyal to their employers. Many left and went their own way, but Lee Ping's nature and dreams of home and making his family proud, would not let him break the agreement. He would carry on.

He enjoyed the kookaburras laughing at dusk and the bellbirds calling to their mates. It was so special when he came out of his tent in the morning and was surrounded by wallabies nibbling on the grass. These small things kept him from going mad.

When Lee emerged from the tunnel, the sun was blinding. His eyes were red and sore from the dust and grit that was in the thick, dry air. His body was on fire. His thirst could not be quenched by the warm water from his drink bottle, so he headed to the Golden Nugget. It had been a hard day. He needed his mind to be taken away to a different place.

Tonight, the undernourished bar maid was standing in front of him asking what she could do for him. She smiled. Lee Ping saw Mu's face smiling right there in this far away land. He reached out to touch her. She felt so soft it made Lee's hand tingle. There was no way Lee could not take the comfort he was looking for. And Jane Barlow was ready to satisfy Lee's desires, for the reward of a hearty meal.

It was late when Lee left the Nugget. His tent was at the far end of town, so he had to walk through the crowded main street. There was always noise and activity going on and it was a hangout for people looking to steal whatever they could find to escape this hell hole. It wasn't easy to find your way to the city and survive without money. It was not the best place to be late at night. There was always someone looking for an easy way out.

Lee pushed his wages deep inside his shirt and headed into the night. His emotions were drained. Lee was a shadow of himself lost. He was walking but he felt nothing under his feet or any feeling of the night air on his face. He could not hear his heartbeat. The loss of dignity and the will to go on.

He never noticed the two men that had followed him. When they jumped him from behind, he was so surprised that it took him a minute to respond. It also surprised him that he wanted to fight for his life. He still wanted to get home to his beloved China, but he was no match for these two well-fed brutes.

They left him where he lay behind a deserted camp sight just off the main street, Lee Ping stared into the darkness and into nothing.

His body was found late the next afternoon Lee was almost unrecognisable stripped of every belonging that was usable to anyone that had passed by. Large ravenous black birds clustered over the corpse, enjoying his remains. They had taken his eyes, but his spirit would rise, to be left in Ravens Hollow for eternity.

Mu Ping had always known when she said goodbye to Lee, she would never see him again. The letter from the company had said Lee Ping from Shanghai, China, had died from a chest complaint on the Victorian Gold Fields. The letter said he was a credit to the company and should be regarded with great pride by his family. The small amount of money that came with the letter did not lessen Mu's grief. Mu would never know the true story behind Lee's death.

Lee Ping would watch with sightless eyes the greed, the fraud, the tragedies and the further exploitation of his countrymen. He watched the growth of the township, the building, the tents being replaced by cottages, fires sweeping through the streets, causing destruction and death. He would watch hundreds come and go, some becoming rich, some becoming poorer, the growth of stores and hotels everywhere. It became a bustling town.

Lee Ping's voice could be heard on the darkest nights, full of isolated agony. Lee watched and waited as time would create a community of lost souls that floated into the abyss. Gathering them together, embracing them without judgement with open arms. To his new family, his true nature would become evident as a loyal and supportive leader through eternity.

He watched with tears in his sightless eyes as that scrawny barmaid gave birth to his son.

2

LEE PING WATCHES WITH SIGHTLESS EYES: BUILDING THE BONES OF RAVENS HOLLOW

Irreverent to the Faith, Gustav Schmidt had convinced his wife Elva along with their two boys Dirk and Karl, to take the journey to Australia.

He had heard of the gold. This place could satisfy his thirst for wealth, along with his pursuit to spread the word of the Lord and gather a congregation of disciples. He would build a congregation that would feed his ego and prove his worth to his God and family. Gustav would be following in his father's footsteps, but well out of the sight of his judgemental eyes.

After a long and exhausting journey from their homeland, they approached Ravens Hollow. Black birds circled around the coach, contrasted against the bright cobalt blue of the clear sky. It was dazzling, making a surreal back drop for the Sentinels to perform their routine. As the birds flew around them, their wings fluttering and soaring above their heads, their shrill voices seemed to speak to Gustav. He took this as a message from the Holy Spirit. This is where he would spread the word and become The Preacher.

Elva took it as a sign of impending disaster.

They set-up on the edge of town on the north end of the main street, where most of the activity was to be seen. The Mining Exchange always had a small group collecting the pennies from their diggings. Gold was harder to come by now. The big companies had almost stripped the land bare. Gustav erected two tents. They were to become their home and the first protestant church in Ravens Hollow.

Gustav was happy to preach to anyone who passed by. The ones that listened and the ones that didn't, the ones that believed and the ones that didn't. He would preach to the air if he had to. That was the whole purpose. That is why he existed. God is good, God will provide. He gave no thought to the family's needs, never gave any thought to how the food got on the table.

Elva cried and begged; the boys stole. That's how the food got on the table in Elva's mind. God had nothing to do with it. They tried to get help from Gustav, the man that was supposed to provide for his family. Blinded by his faith, the father and husband believed God would fill that role.

Elva cried for her lost country and longed to be home in a civilised world. She missed the snow on the mountain peaks, swimming in the lakes in the summer and the music, oh! The music, the history that surrounded her village and the bustling cities.

She would never see that history in this country. She was going to be part of the history of this place, but wanted no part of it. Begging Gustav to spend some of the money he had been accumulating to build his church, for a family cottage so they could be warm in the winter and cool in the summer. The family was always sick with coughs and colds. It was a miserable existence.

The snakes and spiders and all manner of insects invaded their tent, scaring Elva every day. She was always screaming for the boys to help her. If they were away at the small school that had been set-up for the miner's children, she would just hold her breath until the creatures moved on.

Elva hated Gustav. She didn't believe in his God, or any of his ideals. She saw the hypocrisy of his sanctimonious ranting and ravings. But she hated herself more for her weakness, for being taken in by his charm and his mesmerising words.

He played with her soul owning it, Gustav had ways of touching her that took her breath away. Looking at her, she would do anything to please him. How could she ever live without him?

'Tell the preacher you love him, then he will give you what you want.'

Well… Elva never did get what she wanted and now he had brought her to this place, making her leave her mother, father and sister and her beloved country, visions she was finding hard to recall now. It all seemed so long ago. Her depression was so deep her children didn't even bring a smile to her face. She wished she had the courage to kill Gustav. Elva cried.

There are souls that never feel the warmth of another.

Martha and Violet had been in the orphanage since they were born. They knew no other life. Neither knew anything about their heritage or where they came from. They had no one else but each other.

They pretended to be sisters, but the likelihood seemed remote. Martha was dark, with big brown eyes and a smile that could melt hearts. Violet had red hair and freckles and was very shy, hiding behind Martha most of the time. Martha was the smart one. Born under different circumstances, success would have been hers for the asking.

Violet idolised Martha and would have followed her to the end of the world. Together, they gave each other the strength they needed to exist and survive the misery of the orphanage. They had never known any other life, but knew there must be a better way, from things they had heard and read.

When Martha was fourteen, assuming Violet was about the same age, they would put the plan they had devised into action and escape. They had heard about the gold in Central Victoria. Everyone was getting rich there, so that was where they were going to head.

Every week, two girls had to take the vegetables that had been grown at the orphanage to the local store for resale. The girls had to take the money straight back to the matron, so their plan had to be streamlined because they wouldn't have long to disappear with the money.

When it was their time to go to the store, they were ready. The girls put the few belongings they had in the bottom of the baskets and left the only home they had ever known without a backward glance. Putting the money in their shoes and headed west. Staying off the roads and climbed through the thickest scrub they could find. Because they had taken the money, the police would hunt for them longer than for the kids that had left with nothing.

If they were caught, they would be doomed. The matron could not tolerate thieves. Their lives would be unbearable, so they had to move fast. They stole eggs, vegetables, fruit and anything else edible. Washing where they could, in puddles and creeks. Cleanliness was the one thing the matron had embedded in their minds, but by the time they reached the gold fields their hair was matted and their clothes were rags. They'd lost so much weight they looked like ten-year-olds. Never spending any of the money they had stolen in fear of being caught. So, the first stop was to find somewhere they could wash and rest. The Sentinels let them through without a sound, just a sorrowful look. Knowing the girls' fate was sealed.

Tilly spotted them as soon as they came up the main street. A clean-up and a few feeds and they would make her a pretty profit. She wasn't sure if they were too young, but some liked them that way. She ran her Happy Place as she called it, from detached rooms beside The Golden Nugget.

The only entry was from the back lane. There was a cute shop front with lace curtains hiding the ugliness behind. The front door was always bolted. Most locals knew what lay behind. The women were sure their husbands and sons never went near Tilly's. It was just for the lonely miners that had left their families behind on their pursuit for riches.

The girls were so naïve; they thought nothing could be as bad as the orphanage. When Tilly offered them a room for a little of their money their dream was coming true. Tilly groomed the girls for a few weeks. Martha was so attractive she was sure she would be very popular with her clients. Violet wasn't as saleable, but Tilly would make her work for her keep.

It wasn't long before the girls realised Tilly was going to exploit them, but she told them they would earn plenty of money, so how hard could it be?

Martha had never known such fear as the night Tilly said she was sending one of her best clients to her room and he was paying extra because she was a virgin. So, she must be nice to him and do everything he asked of her.

Martha had no idea what any of this meant. She was trembling when a tall, handsome man entered the room. Martha detected a strange accent when he asked her name, but she couldn't speak, so never answered, trying to keep her eyes and mouth closed. He came close to her, taking her cold and trembling hand.

'This will be a wonderful thing you are doing. It is God's will,' he said in a whisper. Martha may have been ignorant to what men's needs were, but she knew this was not right.

'Just tell the preacher you love him and then he will give you what you want.' His smooth voice echoed in her ears.

His strange accent made her recoil. Her mind was in turmoil. She was screaming inside. Suddenly he was ripping at her clothes. 'Come on girl, get out of those rags you are wearing.' She looked at his hands groping at her breast. His fingernails were long, with a line of black dirt under every nail. She thought she would vomit. She couldn't fight. He brought his mouth down on hers. She felt his teeth biting into her lips and his saliva running down her throat. The smell of the sweat on his undershirt mixed with his tobacco breath was taking her breath away. He was hurting her; pulling at her untouched body, slapping her, touching her with those long filthy fingers, yelling at her, 'Tell the preacher you love him, tell the preacher you love him,' over and over. She finally got the words out. He grinned. 'That's a good girl. Now I will give you what you want.'

Martha felt something go through her like a burning poker. She was sure she would die. He was lying on top of her. His weight had the heaviness of a corpse. He wasn't moving. She wanted to cry; she wanted to scream; she wished and prayed she would die.

Tilly said the preacher was happy with her and would call on her again. Martha hoped the bruises all over her body would have a chance to heal before she had to endure his abuse again. Martha was so upset she had brought Violet into this world of abuse and violation, but she couldn't see how they could escape. They cried in each other's arms every night as they shared the stories of the horrors they experienced during their times with Tillie's clients and longed for the misery of the orphanage.

Martha hated the preacher so much. He was demanding and always left bruises and scratches all over her body. She tried to hide her injuries from Violet. The sound of Violet's sobbing in the night was unbearable; she didn't want to add to her misery. Martha wished she had the courage to kill the preacher. Some of the men were kind to her, something she had not experienced before in her life. Those days were easier to cope with, and sometimes the girls giggled over some of the men's antics.

Martha woke with severe pains in her stomach. They had been in Ravens Hollow about eight months and were learning to accept their place in society. They knew this life was all they could hope to achieve. Their room was nice enough and the food was good. Tilly did look after her girls.

When the pain became extreme, Martha crept down the stairs so she wouldn't wake Violet. Trying not to scream, she lay in the alley behind the buildings. The lamps were all out and the clouds had blocked any moonlight that may have crept through. It was the darkest night.

Tilly had suspected Martha may have been pregnant. She was a light sleeper, so hearing the groaning in the alley, she knew what was going on. Taking a blanket, she ran down the stairs to the alley, towards Martha's agonised moaning.

With a beginning, there will be an end.

Eventually, Gustav got his church. A building with a coloured glass window, Jesus hanging on a cross, sending a kaleidoscope of symbolic patterns around the church with the rise and fall of the sun.

How could something so beautiful be so horrible? Elva hated the window. Even though she received three small rooms behind the church, she had pleaded with Gustav not to spend the money on the window and let her have an indoor stove with a chimney. But he wouldn't hear of it, saying the gas ring she had was adequate, and any way she could always build a fire outside if she wanted to. Elva cried.

They had only been in the new building for a short time when Elva woke at dawn to hear whimpering coming from the front of the church. It sounded like more trouble for Gustav to deal with. That would be his problem. She would go back to sleep. Little did she know this baby would bring meaning to her wasted life.

Gustav knew the baby was his as soon as he opened the door and knew Tilly would have moved Martha and Violet on. He would not be asking any questions.

Is this the only purpose of one's life to give the gift of life to another?

As the baby slipped from Martha's body, Martha took her last breath. Tilly had to work fast. This had to be all cleaned up before daylight. She dragged the body to the side of the alley and pushed it over into the deep gully that ran the length of the main street at the back of the buildings. The thick undergrowth quickly swallowed Martha into her grave.

Now Tilly had to take care of Violet. She didn't have to think twice. Violet would ask too many questions. She knew what she had to do. She crept into the girl's room. Violet was still sleeping. She took Martha's pillow and held it hard over Violet's face. She didn't even struggle, as if she had no will to live. It didn't take long to get the job done. Tilly thought maybe she did the girl a favour.

Somehow, she managed to get the body down to the side of the gully. It was hard to see where she had pushed Martha in. For some reason, she felt as though they should be together. She had to use all her strength to get Violet to lie with her sister. The branches, leaves, grass and rubble seemed to open like the mouth of the grim reaper, swallowing Violet. It was a shame, Tilly thought, she had started to like the girls, but business was business. She had to look after her reputation. There was no room for family affairs in Tilly's world.

The force of survival.

The baby's face was his face. He hoped no one else would see it.

He told Elva the baby was a gift from God and she was sent to them to bring joy into their lives. *Just more work for me*, Elva thought, but when she saw the girl, it was love at first sight. Gustav named her Mary. Elva wanted to argue but decided to call her Doll when he wasn't around. And that was what she became to Elva, her baby doll.

The boys had kept her alive, but Doll gave her a reason to live. Elva never thought anyone could have filled the emptiness like a gaping hole in her heart that the years of hating Gustav had left her to deal with the best she could. It was incredible to everyone in the town Elva and the boys didn't realise the girl was Gustav's illegitimate child.

He paraded Mary around town on his shoulders. He didn't think people would suspect he was her real father. Being a respected spiritual leader of the community, he was just doing the Lord's work, giving the poor child a home.

For the first time, the Schmidt family seemed to be happy. The boys laughed with Mary, and Elva smiled. She never thought about Doll's heritage, just thought some poor unfortunate girl got herself into trouble and her family couldn't face the shame. Sometimes she caught a smile she was sure she had seen before, but just couldn't place it.

The boys were working now. Maybe there would be enough money for a proper stove and chimney. Doll would be home from school soon, so Elva thought she would put the soup on and have a lie down before she had to face the trauma of the evening meal.

She didn't wake until the flames were filling the kitchen and racing towards the bed. Smoke was filling her lungs. She had to get out quickly. Moving swiftly towards the door of the church, she was suffocating. She fell to the floor just as the beautiful, horrible, coloured glass window exploded. She smiled, knowing Gustav would mourn his window more than her. Before the darkness engulfed her, she was sure she heard her mother call. Elva cried.

Lee Ping's community was growing. Martha's groans and Violet's sobbing could be heard on the darkest nights. Their entwined bones would not be found until the next century, when the gully was turned into a huge concrete drain. Heavy rain would fill the bluestone gutters and flood the roads and low-lying buildings. This modern engineering accomplishment would control the water that rushed down the hill from one end of town to the other. The bones left of Martha and Violet were buried under the concrete. No one cared.

Elva's screams could be heard every time she heard the preacher say, 'Tell the preacher you love him and he will give you what you want.'

Lee Ping would watch as Dirk married Mary, still not knowing she was his sister. They would produce healthy children and the family grew and grew. The stories of Gustav and Elva faded and were forgotten. When Hitler and the Third Reich were destroying the world, the Schmidts had become the Smiths and the next generations lost all knowledge of their German heritage.

Gustav Schmidt's name was wiped from every record Ravens Hollow had. The church was burned to the ground without a trace of it ever being there. Dirk, Kurt and Mary wanted it that way. The weight of the cross was lifted from their shoulders.

3

MABEL BURNS, NURSE AT YOUR SERVICE: A CALLING TO HEAL

Mabel was a poor kid living with her mother and father behind a butcher's shop in a Melbourne slum area. The rooms were damp and gloomy. A hessian curtain at the end of the small kitchen hid Mabel's bed. There was a sofa, a wooden table and two wooden chairs. Also crammed into the same area, the other room was her parent's bedroom.

Mabel wanted more out of life and prayed one day she would find a better way. Clive was the butcher's son. They had another two rooms above the shop as their living quarters. Mabel and Clive were best friends and spent most of their childhood talking about how to make money and escape their unfavourable circumstances. They had many plans and dreams they really knew would never be a reality. But making plans seemed to turn their mundane existences around, taking them to different and exciting places.

Clive's father expected him to go into the business and go down the same path he had taken. Clive was going to find it hard to let his father down. Somehow, he would have to get the courage. He was relying on Mabel's strength to push him through it. His mother had died many years ago, so they had worked hard, father and son, against the world.

Mabel's father was a drunk and never was any help to the family. Her mother scrubbed and cleaned from early morning until late into the night to pay the rent and put bread and milk on the table, and of course, to keep the beer money flowing. Mabel would never choose that life for herself. There had to be a better world out there somewhere and, along with Clive, she was going to find it.

It was a normal morning when fate stepped in. Mabel was around thirteen and just about to go off to school, when her mother called to her from her bed. She was too sick to go to work and asked Mabel would she be able to go for her, as she didn't want to lose one of her best jobs.

The doctor's rooms were a few streets away. Mabel ran and was puffing hard, being a little overweight. When she entered the waiting room, she just wanted to sit down. Before she had a chance, the doctor came out calling for her mother, 'She is sick today. She sent me to do her job,' Mabel said shyly. Expecting to be given a broom, Mabel had no idea what was going to confront her.

She was horrified by what she saw. Her whole body was shaking. Her hands trembled as she did what she was told, hoping she could get out quickly and try to forget. There were six more women the doctor operated on before she could leave.

Each woman thanked the doctor with such gratitude and handed him a roll of money. She didn't really understand what was going on and was not sure her mother was going to tell her. Mabel assumed this was where most of their money was coming from. When she was leaving, the doctor gave her a note to take home to her mother.

'The doctor said you did a very good job and you have a natural talent for nursing. He would like you to work for him if you would like.' Her Mother read the note proudly.

Mabel couldn't believe she had a job and she could leave school. She was not sure it was a dream job, but it was a job, so she would make the best of it. Mabel's mother said she could have a little of the money and she would get another cleaning job. Mabel didn't ask any questions. She decided she would watch and listen and learn as she went. She would be scared to death, but she would have money. Maybe her dreams could come true one day.

Mabel just couldn't wait to tell Clive. He knew all about abortion, and it was against the Hippocratic Oath doctors took. Doctors pledged to save lives, not to destroy one before it began. Mabel only saw the relief on the women's faces after the operation. Even if the pain was strong and their shame stronger, they went away happy.

Clive was impressed with the money, so became interested after all. It was the woman's choice, and it was her body someone had probably taken advantage of anyway. And the conditions were clean and sterilised. It was better than going to a dirty backyard, unqualified old woman, or doing it themselves. So many had died from trying to get rid of unwanted pregnancies. Clive convinced himself it really was a noble service.

They saved as much money as they could. Mabel worked alongside her doctor, and Clive, his father. Mabel was sixteen and Clive nineteen when they had enough money to get married and move on. To their surprise, everyone was happy for them. Mabel's mother and Clive's father were sad to see them go, but were very proud of them. No one else from either family had been able to escape the slums. They wished them all the best for their adventure.

Mabel and Clive planned to travel and find a place without medical care and set up a practice giving general first aid. Of course, Mabel would be there with her extra talent to help a poor girl that had got herself into trouble, or some poor woman who had had too many children. So that was the way they went. They were happy and carried their belongings in their dray. Their faithful pony, Bobby, was happy to pull their load. It was always easy to find a place to rent in most small towns especially, in towns where the gold had run out and people had moved on to a new strike.

Mabel had grown into a large young woman with humongous breasts that jumped around like oversized balloons when she laughed, which she did much of the time. Her jovial nature put people at ease at the times when they were most in need of Mabel's help. Clive was just the opposite—tall, skinny and a little sombre. They were overjoyed to have each other. They did good everywhere they went. As the years went by, their only disappointment was that they were never blessed with children. They both decided it was their punishment for stopping so many babies from entering the world.

When they felt their work was done, or a doctor moved into town, they would load up the dray, Bobby's holiday would be over and off they would go. Clive would have checked out new areas ahead of time, so they had their accommodation sorted before they arrived. They needed a room for Mabel to see her patients, with somewhere to eat and sleep, and it was always good to have a wash house with a wood burning copper. Clive oversaw boiling everything that belonged to them. They were saving their money, of which there was plenty. Keeping her paper wealth folded deep inside the folds of Mabel's humongous breasts. It was for the day they found a place they wanted to stay and settle down and maybe give up their work.

They were relaxing after dinner, as usual. Mabel was chatting away, telling Clive about who she had met and helped during her day. She didn't notice Clive wasn't making any comments. He was always interested in Mabel's work. She had had a day full of satisfied patients, so she was in high spirits, almost singing as she told her stories. 'So, tell me, Clive, how was your day?' she asked, still singing away. It took her a minute to realise he didn't answer. Mabel looked over at Clive and froze.

He was sitting there dead. Who dies before they are thirty for no reason? Mabel couldn't move. She couldn't cry out for help; she was the help. She sat and stared at him for hours. This could not be happening. Why would it? He would wake up soon.

Mabel sat and watched Clive for two days. Her heart was broken. She had loved Clive for as long as she could remember. Maybe she could stop breathing too. On the third day, she knew she would have to do something but letting him go was unbearable.

It was some time before she started to see patients again. That was what Clive would have wanted her to do. She thought if he was watching, that would make him proud of her. It gave her some comfort in a way, to keep going. So that is what she did, just as if Clive was by her side.

She had heard about an empty cottage in a neighbouring mining village and was ready for a new start. She had to retire the old faithful Bobby, who wouldn't have been able to make another journey pulling Mabel's load. Bobby's replacement (Bobby 2) helped get Mabel to her next destination. She chuckled to herself as she wondered why she couldn't replace Clive as easily.

Mabel Burns was going grey now and was as round as she was high. Her humongous bosom had become half her person and her smile was now missing a couple of teeth she had to extract when she couldn't stand the pain any longer.

With her rosy cheeks and her toothless smile, she would still charm everyone that crossed her path. She still was impressive in her starched white, well-pressed uniform, she now had to take care of herself. It had always been Clive's job. She could have been going to work in a Melbourne hospital. She had only spent a short time there to pass her Nursing Certificate some time back. The doctor had trained her well.

The night was closing in when they reached the outskirts of her new town. The ravens gathered. Bobby 2 slowed. Mabel looked up to the sky and watched as the ravens flapped their wings around her head. She listened to the sentinels choir of enthusiastic shrieks as they parted and let them through. Mabel did not know the significance of the performance but took it as a positive omen all the same.

Bobby 2's legs were trembling under the load. Mabel and her chattels on the old two wheeled dray exhausted him. He was looking forward to his respite and hoped he would be ready for Mabel's next move when the time came. When they got to the cottage, the moon was leading the way.

Mabel had settled Bobby 2 into his paddock and was walking back to the cottage when she nearly fell into an unused underground concrete well. It was lucky the moon was shining, she thought. Or was Clive with her tonight? Either way, she could have ended up at the bottom of the empty, great hole. She had a good feeling about her stay in Ravens Hollow.

The next day, Mabel nailed her rustic sign onto the post and rail fence: NURSE MABEL BURNS AT YOUR SERVICE.

There hadn't been a doctor in the Hollow for some time. Doctors also followed the gold. There was still wealth and riches to be found everywhere, but human greed would rise up and most followed the new richer strikes.

The population wasn't at its height now. There were some empty buildings with merchants moving on too. There had been six hotels at the peak of the rush; now there were only three. The Golden Nugget was still the first port of call for most of the Born and Bred and the blow-ins alike. Mabel had called in to stock up on her nightly nip of brandy, 'Just to keep the heart bouncing,' she would tell Clive, if he thought she had had too much. Of course, everyone stared at this person, newly arrived in their realm. Mabel knew it wouldn't be long before most would have a reason to head to her door.

Mabel set to getting everything clean and cutting back overgrown branches and grass from the pathway to her door. It had always been harder without Clive, but she amazed herself at the jobs she had to do that she had relied on him for in the past. But that was the way it was, so she just got on with it. Most days were very busy. She was so tired by the end of the day that she fell asleep, not having time to miss Clive at all. The townsfolk had had to rely on home remedies and primitive first aid for their illness and injuries. Mabel had chosen a town in need.

Her first weeks were full of coughs and colds, scratches and bruises. They were testing her. She was getting to know who among them had true grit and who were the 'would bees if they could bees,' that looked down their noses at what they would consider low life. Mabel treated everyone with the same care and chit-chat.

Sometimes she made a friend, but that wasn't very important to her. When she had Clive, she never tried to encourage any outside acquaintances at all. Now though, without the only person other than her mother she had loved, when she got lonely, she learned to gain solace through her patients.

Mabel became an important member of the community. She had a potion for most of the common ailments and complaints. If she didn't, she would take a punt and make something up, either with medicine or advice. Her treatments, advice or the suggestions that their symptoms would vanish with her care, usually worked.

She was everyone's friend. She never judged. They began to rely on her for their peace of mind. They felt safe having her on their side. Mabel shouldered her job well. She was their 'Nightingale'.

Her services were rewarded with a variety of useful goods, as well of plenty of cash or gold. The bigger the secret she had to keep, the bigger the reward. The children were always happy with the sweets she handed out. The tired women were grateful for a hug from her roly-poly soft arms, squeezing them to her heart surrounded by those humongous breasts.

She turned a blind eye when the men thought they had secretly touched those unbelievable bosoms. She knew they would boast about it at the pub later. It just made her giggle. They had never really been touched by anyone but Clive. Mabel was enjoying her stay in the Hollow. She would be sad when the day came that she would leave this place where she was so needed. But she knew one day things would change nothing is forever good or bad.

Mabel's extra talent became well known. It was employed many times, especially for the girls too young and the women too old to be mothers. Nobody seemed to notice the young girls that came to Mabel's door after dark and left twenty minutes later trembling with their heads low.

Mabel disposed of the fetuses late at night. The old well was a Godsend and with her trusty bucket of lime powder, all was gone and forgotten. She never left the well without repeating a prayer: 'Dear Sweet Mother, take this little soul and keep it for another day.'

Joy came to Mabel when she delivered a beautiful, healthy baby. Watching the mother taking her newborn into her arms was something that always amazed her and brought tears to her eyes. There were many sad days she had to cope with and some horrific injuries and traumas too hard for the knowledge she had. But she was never ashamed of how she handled what was confronting her. She just did her best. She had some lucky escapes and didn't always know why things worked. Mabel was grateful at the end of the day if her work had been done well.

Mabel woke to hear her door rattling. It was after midnight. She instinctively knew it was going to be bad. She opened the door to four white fearful eyes; their dark skin couldn't be seen in the shadows. Uneasiness washed over Mabel. The blacks never came to her. They had their own methods and their elders that ruled over the tribes. If there was a problem, they always handled it themselves. Her guess was the pair had been shunned and couldn't get the help they needed. They were far too young to be parents. Mabel's first instinct was to turn them away, but her compassion was going to be her downfall. She had to help if it was in her power. The eeriness in the air was unnerving and she didn't feel like her invincible self.

The girl was in labour and severe pain. What else could she do but try to bring her magic to the fore? She asked the boy to stay outside and ushered the girl through the linen and lace curtain that hung over the door that separated the rooms. It was Mabel's symbol of how far she had come from her childhood days of staring though the hessian curtain that hid her bed from the world.

Mabel lit the lamp and laid the lass down on the clean bed she had prepared for the next day. Looking at the girl in the light, it was clear she was far too young to be a mother, or dead, which was looking like a possibility. Her pain became Mabel's pain too and they worked together, almost becoming one against the agony and fear of the unknown.

Two hours later, the baby was born. That was when Mabel made her big mistake. She saw immediately the baby's spine was twisted, but was not quick enough to stop the baby's cry. She stopped its breathing so fast that she hoped neither the boy nor girl had heard the sound. Mabel said to the couple she was so sorry the baby did not survive and maybe the girl should rest for a while before they moved on.

The girl was crying and asking why she had heard the baby cry. Mabel assured her she must have imagined it and convinced them, because of the hard labour the baby did not have the strength to live and was born dead. The boy was anxious to leave. Looking relieved, he wanted to get away and be shot of the whole affair. He pulled the girl to him and kept saying, 'It was for the best,' dragging her away, telling her it was her imagination. He never heard a baby cry and she was too stressed and scared to know what had happened.

Mabel didn't have a lot of time. She had so much to do. She wanted to be out of the Hollow before daylight. She hurried to the well, putting the tiny body down gently, repeating her prayer for the last time in Ravens Hollow. 'Dear sweet mother, take this little soul into your heart and save it for another day'. Throwing the last bucket of lime into the grave, she then shovelled as much dirt into the well as she could manage.

She hurried to get Bobby 2 from the paddock and hitch him to the dray, throwing her belongings on as fast as she could. Half an hour later she was ready to go, checking all her wealth was neatly folded in the safety deposit chest that was beginning to sag somewhat. But she knew no one would find it there.

Mabel felt she had little choice. If the young ones had not been from a local tribe, she may have taken a chance. She had heard many stories about the pointing of the bone. She was afraid she might become a victim. Knowing the curse of vengeance was only a suggestion (much like her medicine), gave her no comfort. She had lost. She knew she had done the right thing and saved the young ones from a life of pain, but she had to leave. There was no other way.

As they headed out of town, the light from the full moon caught the tears running down Mabel's cheeks. She had done her best. She knew there would be a successor and she would be soon forgotten. Little did she know, the town of Ravens Hollow would not soon forget her.

The cottage would be known as Mabel Burns Cottage long after her makeshift sign fell off the fence. There would be a new sign erected by the community. They didn't want to forget her roly-poly body and cheerful nature. She would find another town in need where her sense of purpose would be rekindled. If only Clive was at her side…

The sentinels lined the road, with their heads bowed, Mabel's guard of honour. The black ravens didn't make a sound. She chuckled and blew them a kiss.

Lee Ping watched with sightless eyes and welcomed the baby to join his community. The cries would be heard every full moon. It was a long time before anyone could bear to stay in the cottage. The baby's cries would drive them away.

4

THE HARTNELLS

Raylene had fallen in love with Jim, or maybe it was the promises he made for a new, exciting life, far away from her miserable existence.

Jim was what every poor girl dreamed of. He was tall, with the strongest arms she had ever seen. When he spoke, his deep, smooth voice made her head spin. His words were so worldly and knowing, to Raylene anyway. He sweet-talked her into believing every word he said. She fell under his spell with ease. She was looking for a way out; getting away from her abusive father and a mother that had never known how to love her. She had been working towards her escape for years. Her parents were the saddest pair and she had inherited their unhappiness. She was sure if she could only get away, she would feel like a new person. Jim Hartnell was the answer.

Lee Ping watched with sightless eyes as the Sentinels let them through with a soothing song. Were they feeling Raylene's pain and didn't look closely at Jim?

To play the role you were appointed.

The Victorian Public Health Department was opening a tuberculosis sanitorium in the Hollow. Ravens Hollow had seen a stream of doctors come and go since Mabel Burns. It was the hope of the townsfolk that there would be a permanent doctor in the growing town. Now, with a new modern building with fifty beds, there was hope a doctor would stay.

Dr Theo Diamond would oversee the sanitorium with Theo's wife, Meredith, looking after the nursing staff. The sanitorium would mainly be palliative care, allowing Theo to have time to set-up a private practice in their small cottage just off the main street. He would use the front room, erecting a door in the passage to separate the living quarters. The small orchard in the back yard made the move to Ravens Hollow comfortable and inviting. It seemed a perfect place. They were looking forward to making it the permanent home for their children, Oscar and Hilda, and becoming part of the community. Little did they know how hard it would be.

All was going well with their medical pursuits. The sanitorium was always busy. Theo did his rounds there twice a day. Few left the sanitorium regaining their health to return to their families. It was a sad place, but Meredith handled the work with ease.

In the first few months, Theo only saw accidents and emergencies in his practice. He passed the trial period and soon the locals were making a steady stream to his door with all their woes and problems large and small. If only they could be accepted as Ravens Hollow's locals, they would be happy.

He heard stories of Mabel Burns and how loved she had been, becoming a folk hero. He imagined the stories had grown over time. There was no one left that really knew her, but he wished he could have been sprinkled with a little of her magic.

Father Brenden O'Neil came to town about a year after the Diamonds. He had been moved around frequently since he had become a priest; never fitting in well to any Catholic community, never building up a reasonable number of parishioners to fill the church pews. He came to the Hollow feeling it would be a short stay and expected to be moved on again. He was never sure whether it was the communities or the priesthood he had the problem with. Maybe he wasn't cut out to be a priest. He tried and would keep trying. Ravens Hollow might be the place in which he could make a difference and shine.

Theo and Brenden soon became friends, both being outcasts, never being invited to any gatherings or community affairs. Meredith and the children were shunned too. They were all there to help this unforgiving place and this was their reward.

Theo and Brenden talked over their problems with a bottle of wine most nights, sometimes making plans to break down the barriers that divided them from their patients and parishioners. Some nights they talked into the wee hours of the morning, Brenden walking home in the moonlight listening to the strange sounds of the Hollows night. They knew the reason for the community keeping them in their place and not letting them in to their social lives, but had no idea how to solve this social dilemma.

The people they had spoken to and helped the day before would cross the street with their heads turned away, red faced, rather than look them in the eye and say hello.

Theo and Brenden knew all the community's secrets, crimes, weaknesses, who they hated, who they loved, their embarrassments, their private moments, their hopes and dreams. The division between helpers and the needy was a gap almost impossible to overcome.

When the two outcasts talked over their wine, the conversations were always hypothetical. Never a name was mentioned. They were true to the oath they had taken. They were loyal to their professions. At the end of the night, they always put it down to the enigma of human nature and would sit back and watch as the jigsaw became part of the pattern of the growing town they hoped to become accepted into in time. It was true Theo and Brenden were part of the structure that held the community together. That was the role they had to play.

The wonder of dreaming, shattered dreams.

Theo helped Raylene through her first confinement. When the Hartnell's first son came into the world, Raylene called him William, but Jim would always call him Billy. Jim had enough odd jobs around the town to keep food on the table of the small cottage they had managed to buy with Raylene's savings. It was money she had hidden away for the day she would escape from her parents. She was so proud of her little home and family. William was all she could have hoped for. She poured all the love she had into him.

Jim started to come home drunk. Raylene just thought he was doing too many jobs down at the Nugget. Jim knew he was losing. The spell he had held over her was becoming weaker. Now Billy was coming before him and his needs and he didn't like it. He started to stay away and came home as late as he could, hoping Raylene and the kid would be asleep. He was having all his fun at the Nugget anyway. Raylene didn't care if he left her alone; she had William now.

In time, Jim did come home and demanded the comfort a wife was required to provide. If Raylene was asleep, it didn't matter, he just took what he wanted. She often woke with him slapping her, ripping at her clothes, punching her on her back. Jim came to like taking Raylene this way. The more violent he was, the more he enjoyed it and this new power. She had escaped one miserable life for another. William was the only joy she knew. Rape was a new horror for her. Most times, the bruises could be covered by clothes or make up. If not, she would stay indoors for a few days.

It wasn't long before Theo was helping Raylene through another birth. This one wasn't so easy. Theo suggested she shouldn't have another pregnancy too soon. Another boy. Raylene called him Herbert. Jim called him Bertie. Raylene loved Herbert just as much as William.

Jim just kept harping on about having a girl. Next time it will be a girl. Raylene tried to explain to Jim that Dr Diamond had said it would be dangerous for her to have another baby too soon, but he didn't listen. He didn't care.

Douglas, who Jim called Dougie was the next; then came James, who Jim called little Jimmy. 'We will have a girl the next time,' Jim kept saying. Raylene just wanted to stay alive to look after her babies.

Theo pleaded with her to talk to Jim and tell him her life was in danger and that another baby would kill her. Theo mentioned tubal ligation and explained it could be done without Jim knowing. Raylene would have to ask Father O'Neil about it. She was sure it wouldn't be allowed.

Theo and Brenden had a heated discussion that night. Without using names, they both knew who they were referring to. Brenden was appalled at the idea Theo could suggest to any patient an operation that could stop a woman producing a child as a solution. Theo tried to explain that if the mother's life was in danger, it would be the right thing to do. Neither could understand the other's point of view. Brenden's purpose was to look after the soul and Theo's was to look after the body. There were so many reasons their ideals and beliefs would never be shared.

Life was busy for both, and they were starting to gain the respect of the locals slowly, some even being a little friendlier.

The next time Raylene became pregnant, Theo talked her into a termination. She just couldn't take the risk of not being there for her children. They needed her. They were growing up fast and getting wilder and wilder. She was so worried they would follow in Jim's footsteps. James was the only one that had a kind nature and had some moral fibre.

Raylene had no idea of how to bring up children, only how to love them. Jim was just a dumb bastard, Raylene now realised, and no better than her father. Jim's strong arms that she had put so much faith in to protect her from harm, had failed her long ago. She was creating a family worse than the one she had come from. She neither had the strength nor the knowledge to change this pending disaster.

Theo hadn't seen Raylene for some time, so was a little surprised to see her come in with a black eye, bruising on her limbs and a cut that had to be stitched. She had fallen on the rough path behind her cottage. Theo believed her, as the injuries fitted her explanation. 'You seem to be losing weight,' Theo commented in the usual patient-doctor banter.

'No, I am fine,' Raylene replied, having no eye contact with him, staring at the floor. Theo was happy she wasn't pregnant. That was the major concern, so wished her well and called in the next patient.

Jim started accusing Raylene of having an affair. That was when he became more violent, so it all started again. Theo saw her more often. He was sure she was being beaten, but somehow Raylene always had an explanation to fit the injuries.

After months of Jim's torture, Raylene was pregnant again. Theo could see Raylene's condition had deteriorated and he was sure she would not survive the next nine months. He suggested the sterilisation operation. Raylene was horrified at the suggestion and knew Father O'Neil would never agree to such a sin. Theo explained the procedure and said they could tell Jim there had been complications with a miscarriage. He was such a dumb bastard, he would never know. It was her life and sanity she was fighting for. She didn't seem to have a choice.

Not long after the operation, Raylene went to confession. The termination weighed heavily on her conscience. Brenden was shocked Theo had gone that far. He found it hard to forgive either Raylene or Theo, even though Raylene explained to him how much easier her life had become.

The drinking discussion that night was not a happy one. It became very heated. There was no tolerance between the friends of either one's point of view.

Jim couldn't understand why Raylene wasn't getting pregnant. He wanted that girl. It wasn't long before the beatings started again. Raylene thought her shame had to be paid for, so she just accepted it. Her life became more miserable than ever, but she owed it to the boys to keep going. She hated Jim now, really hated him. She wished she had the strength to kill him.

She went through each day in a daze, washing their stinking clothes, cooking and cleaning. Never a thank you from anyone, just a sympathetic smile from little Jimmy, who now towered over his dumb bastard of a father. He was the only comfort she had in her life. The other boys were taking after Jim. She had tried so hard to get them educated and into good jobs, but she had failed. They only wanted to drink, smoke and womanise, just like their father. They all had Jim's red hair and freckles, true to their Irish heritage, except little Jimmy. He looked more like Raylene's side; a little darker. She did have a sprinkling of English in her. Billy was girl crazy and brought home any tramp he could find.

The latest was Sheila, a skinny little thing with bad teeth. Billy was crazy about her. She told them her family was poor and considered the Hartnells were living like kings. Raylene didn't understand. Maybe Jim splashed money around that she would never see, probably at the Nugget to big-note himself. He would never give her more than she needed for food and a few clothes.

All the boys worked with Jim. They were kept busy with the odd jobs around the place. There were plenty of new developments going on. The town was expanding and spreading in all directions. The mining had slowed. More were going back to the land and farming was bringing in new wealth. Merchants were moving in and building homes and shops up and down the streets.

Finally, Sheila moved in. The cottage had grown and the boys had built bungalows in the back yard. Only little Jimmy stayed inside with Raylene and Jim, so he was privy to all the goings on. He had to block his ears and try not to get up and kill his father when he could hear his mother being beaten. It was never mentioned the next day. The three of them pretended it never happened.

Jim took a liking to Sheila, always patting Billy on the back, saying what a good choice he made. She was a good sheila, just as her name indicated.

Now Raylene had another mouth to feed, wash and clean for. Sheila was as lazy as the rest. Raylene was their slave. The emptiness she felt was eating away at her. She almost wished for her life with her parents if she could only go back in time.

She visited Theo more often, but never complained about her real problems. She felt at ease with Theo. She knew he would never judge her. The visit took her out of her horror for a small time. Theo never understood the depth of misery she was in. He patronised her somewhat. He had his limitations and his time was taken up with medical needs of the body, not of the mind. A medicine to make her sleep was all he could offer.

Billy and Sheila spent most of their time in the bungalow, but when Sheila came into the house, Jim couldn't take his eyes off her.

'Incestuous bastard,' Jimmy would say to himself. His father made him sick to the stomach. He had heard and seen things all his life that had fuelled his hatred for the brute. He was so scared for his mother, unlike his brothers. They seemed to think Jim was a hero for the way he treated her—a man must keep control, can't let a woman have the upper hand, can't let them think they have equal rights, must make them keep their mouth shut or you'll have to shut it for them. That's the advice he gave the boys. Little Jimmy tried to argue once but got a black eye for his trouble.

Raylene had given up expecting anything but cruelty from Jim, but the day she went to Billy's bungalow to get the laundry her world came tumbling down. She was transfixed at the sight of Jim lying on the bed, making love to Sheila, really making love like she had read about in the romance magazines. She couldn't believe the way he was whispering in her ear, running his hands over her back and gently kissing her neck. He had never treated her with any form of gentleness, even in the early days when she thought they were in love. Sheila was moaning saying how much she loved being in his strong arms and feeling the warmth of his firm body against hers.

Raylene could not believe what she was seeing. This can't be the same man that had raped and beaten her all these years! Never a kind word had he spoken to her. Now here he was, turned into some Romeo over a slut his own son was sleeping with.

Shattered, she slipped out of the bungalow, walked straight to her bedroom, took out the medicine Theo had given her and drank the whole bottle without a second thought. She was being punished for one sin, now she was committing another. No doubt she would pay on the other side.

Her last thought was of little Jimmy. She was letting him down. She tried to remember the joy she felt when she gave birth to her babies, but she couldn't bring it back. It had all gone. There was only the darkness.

Little Jimmy tried to wake her. She was curled up on the floor, clutching the bottle. He hated her for her weakness, but loved her for having the strength to make her own choice and escape at last.

He went to her room to get away from the drunken crowd that was in the living room after the funeral. Sitting on her bed, he saw her crying, asking him to forgive her. She was so sorry she had to leave him. Only wanting peace. She had no understanding of why Jim had treated her so brutally. Raylene promised to watch over him.

Little Jimmy wasn't sure if he was dreaming, though he could feel her presence around him and he could hear the soft weeping and 'Why, why, why?'

Jimmy took on Raylene's role as the carer for the Hartnells and did her work as she had done in the past. His father said women's work suited him. He was such a sissy. So, they began to treat him the same way. He was their slave now. The only comfort he had was when he went into his mother's room and listened to her soft crying, asking, 'Why, why, why?'

Raylene's sobbing would be heard for evermore in Ravens Hollow.

Lee Ping welcomed her to his growing community.

When Sheila realised she was pregnant, she didn't know who the baby's father was, Billy or Jim. It didn't matter much to her, so she let them both think it was theirs. Letting them both support the child. She did this three times. Marlene came first. Jim finally had his daughter; then two boys, Patrick and Morrie, all proving very profitable for Sheila. Jim was happy to pay more because he had Marlene. All having the Hartnell red hair, the girl was more like her mother, a little thing, but the boys were big and strong. Jim had passed on his strength, while Raylene's good nature would never be inherited by any Hartnell offspring. The Hartnell name and sperm would be spread through the district for generations.

Sheila was thrilled with her lot. The games she played with the men worked well for her. She had money in her pocket to do with as she pleased. Little Jimmy did most of the work. As long as she was there when Jim or Billy wanted her, all went smoothly.

The only thing that bothered her was when Raylene appeared. The crying scared her at first and her asking, 'Why, why, why?' Sheila never knew what it meant, but soon became accustomed to it. When she realised Raylene couldn't hurt her, she began to take no notice of the ghost in the corner, crying.

Sheila had no guilt at the deception she played on Raylene's men. She thought they deserved it and she had no fear of revenge from any of them, the dumb bastards!

Theo and Brenden had quite a drinking session after Raylene's suicide. The depth of remorse was engulfing them. Both felt extreme guilt.

They had thought they were helping her get through her struggle, maybe as blindly as they thought they were helping others. Brenden couldn't criticise Theo (even though he didn't agree with the advice he had given her), because he had not healed her soul.

Theo had attempted to heal her body. Maybe in their ignorance, they had done all they could have done. How many others had they played God with, taking their lives in their hands? Why had they given themselves the right? Why had they put themselves in that position.?

Now it would take two bottles of wine to get through their sessions that were becoming more frequent and longer into the night. It was nothing for Meredith to find them both asleep in their chairs in the morning.

Neither ever mentioned they heard Raylene's crying.

In the future, Theo would try to convince Oscar not to choose medicine as a career, but to no avail. There would be more Dr Diamonds in the history of Ravens Hollow. Hilda followed in her mother's footsteps. Medicine was the Diamond's vocation. The sanitorium would eventually grow into the local hospital.

5

BRENDEN O'NEIL CATHOLIC PRIEST: PULLING THE PUPPET'S STRINGS FROM ABOVE

After Raylene's death, Brenden's mind extended into realms it had not explored before. Delving deeper into his consciousness, doubts took shape and became monsters fighting to control the fragile fibre of his soul.

Brenden saw Theo as the Devil's Advocate on their evenings together to stimulate discussion, and he played the game well, but never gave in to anything far from his beliefs. He still had control. The doctrine of his religion was grounded in every fibre of his being. The Catechism was etched into his brain, as if it were the Ten Commandments on Moses' Tablets of Stone, so he could or would not waver. He did not have the capacity to do otherwise.

Brenden's mother prayed with him every night in his childhood. He knew the Rosary before he had gone to school. 'You must love Jesus. He is your father. His word is the truth. If you are bad, He will see and you will be punished.' So, Brenden prayed and was good and his beads were his only friend.

Brenden was a confused child. He was never compatible with any of the other kids. He became known as the boy who was going to be a priest, so was shunned by his peers. The nuns and brothers seemed to revere him, so that gave him some solace. Brenden became content with his world and the love of Jesus. He didn't look to anyone else for consolation or comfort in any way. His mother only wanted him to share the Rosary with her at night before he went to bed, so he learned to be alone with Jesus. That is what he would be: Brenden O'Neil, Catholic Priest, and he would be respected and do good in the world.

Brenden's church stood on the highest rise overlooking the town of Ravens Hollow, the one part of the area that wasn't scarred by the gold mining. It was a modest bluestone building with a large wooden door with a window on each side, taking on the proportions of a face watching the parishioners, watching their sins, keeping them in check. The belltower could be seen from every street. No one could escape the daunting image. On moonlit nights, the moon would shine through the space surrounding the bell. It was like an eye spying on the sinners. The wind would whistle through it, making a haunting sound that echoed across the town like a message that the Lord was watching.

Was this the plan Jesus had laid out for him—to waste away in this ghost of a town? He knew he must have been punished, but for what, he wasn't sure. He had been an obedient servant and followed all the rules. The flocks he gathered were the true faithful. They would have followed any priest that did God's work.

Brenden thought he knew the answers. Obeying bowing down to Jesus and the Pope. He never strayed and this was his reward.

Theo had noticed a change in Brenden. They had been friends for so many years. He almost knew what words would come out of Brenden's mouth before he spoke. Now Brenden was becoming more distant and babbled a lot. Theo had trouble making sense of the debate at times. *We must be getting past it,* Theo thought. *Better cut down on the wine and put his worries aside.* Brenden was fine. He had looked after himself all his life. Why would anything change?

Brenden's mother had died just before he left the seminary. It had caused him little pain. His father had come to his Ordination Service. He shook his hand and said his mother would have been proud and walked away. Brenden wondered whether Shane O'Neil really was his father. It never seemed as though he was, or Sara O'Neil, his mother, for that matter, either. They were both just his carers. God had placed him in their hands, so they would groom him to do His work and spread His word. He was a special person with a special mission. Jesus was his purpose, his passion. He needed no other; his life would be complete. His mind and body were as pure and unadulterated as Jesus himself. Brenden O'Neil was a sinless human being. He became detached from reality. He insulated himself with the protection of the monastic life. A slight, insignificant, colourless Irishman who went unnoticed in the robotic role he filled.

Now his life was filled with a morbid turmoil. He felt he was spiralling into a well of depression and anguish he had no understanding of. He had always known the answers. He had nowhere to go. Brenden had never had to look outside of his faith for anything. He was lost, suffocating, tormented. He knew he was losing his mind.

He heard the voices, the grotesque sounds of the dead. He never believed the stories and rumours about the ones left behind, but he was hearing them all. Sometimes he thought he heard the voice of God, but now it was the sounds of the dead and Raylene calling him to help her, to give her the answer. Brenden didn't know the answers in his ignorance. Always thinking he knew all; and the truth.

Brenden was stumbling subliminally into a new world. Theo's words were starting to have some meaning. He was analysing everything with new interpretation. Taking notice of things he was sure he had never seen before. Being reborn into a world of the masses, the world of the sinner. This world had never been able to touch him before. Jesus had kept him secluded in a religious cocoon. Why was he being thrown out to deal with the devil? Had he lived a lie? His life was a sham. He was a mindless puppet.

Brenden felt like a vulnerable child, drowning in a quagmire of humiliation, hypocrisy, and abandonment. He prayed for help. It never came. He wasn't playing a game anymore; he was facing damnation.

The day he saw her in the second row at the morning service was the beginning of the end. He was caught off guard, something that was new to him. He was always in control. She took his breath away. Her blonde hair fell softly onto her shoulders. Still blue eyes shone, looking up at him with admiration. The pink lips opened and moved into a slight smile. The enigmatic innocence of this young girl stirred feelings through Brenden's body and mind he had never known before. The devil was winning.

Brenden woke in a pool of perspiration. He thought he was on fire. His hands were clutching his huge, pulsating penis. He stared down in horror. What had he done to himself? He knew he had been dreaming about her, the young, beautiful girl. He knew he had his lips resting on hers with his body pressed hard against her. The warmth of her body was electrifying. He was saying, 'I love you; I love you. I love you more than Jesus.' He heard himself screaming.

He could hear his mother's voice saying, 'You must never touch down there. You will go to hell. A priest must never seek pleasures of the flesh.'

Fear took hold of him. His hands strengthened around his cock. He had to get it away. It was growing like a tumour. This monster was sucking the life out of him. Running blindly to the wood pile, he laid his huge pulsating member on the chopping block. He heard the screaming. It seemed far away. It was his voice. 'Fuck you, Sara O'Neil. I curse the day you gave birth to me and sold my soul to the devil, so I could pay penance for your sins. I hate you, you bitch!'

He brought down the axe. His curdling screams echoed across the church yard. 'Jesus Christ, forgive me!'

Theo waited up for his friend, drinking the bottle by himself and falling asleep in his chair. He woke as the dawn light was creeping through the open curtain with an uneasy feeling that something was wrong. Groggy from too much wine and aching from an uncomfortable sleep, he struggled to the kitchen, thinking he would check on Brenden during the day.

It was late in the afternoon. The sun was setting, leaving a mystical glow across the church yard. Theo had called out for Brenden after he got no response from knocking on the open door. He had checked the church before he had gone into the apartment. Theo never knew what sent him to the woodshed. There he discovered his friend lying in a pool of blood, the axe clutched firmly in his hand. Theo took Brenden in his arms and cried. He had let his friend down. How could he ever forgive himself?

Brenden would become one of Lee Ping's disciples now and walk hand in hand with Raylene, both looking for the answer. Screams could be heard across the church yard whenever a pretty, young, blue-eyed blonde girl came and sat in a church pew.

The church bell would ring and Theo would have to have another drink. 'Just for Brenden,' he would say.

6

TOM BARLOW: LEE PING WATCHED HIS SON'S LIFE WITH PRIDE AND SADNESS

When the good are taken there are always others to take their place.

Ruth Barlow, the scrawny barmaid, named the boy Tom. Tom Barlow would become a formidable authoritative member of the community and become a part of the history of Ravens Hollow.

Ruth had left Tom to his own devices almost from the day of his birth. Someone was always there to feed and clean him. The hotel staff and patrons became Tom's family. He never saw a lot of his mother, occasionally, she would step in, giving him a cuddle to lift his spirits. That seemed enough for the both of them to get on with life. She was one of many that influenced and educated Tom through his childhood. He never knew who his father was. Ruth never said. She didn't really know. Lee Ping wasn't the only Chinese miner she had donated her body to for the taking, no questions asked.

Tom wasn't the only child in the Hollow that had oriental features. It was never an issue for him. They all felt like brothers and sisters. He grew up with a freedom not known to many so young. He gained independence and great self-determination.

Tom became a fine young man, joining the Victoria Police Force as soon as he was old enough. He played his role with courage and conviction, earning the respect of all. He had been exposed to many situations that would make most his age recoil in horror, living at the Nugget throughout his childhood. He could have chosen the path of crime just as easily as the law, seeing plenty of criminal acts take place over the years. He honoured his choice with conviction to enforce the law with a rigid and stable authority. He wanted the townsfolk to feel secure and confident under his watch. Tom's pledge was to protect his Ravens Hollow family.

His position in the town was consolidated when he married Queenie Ballard.

Bertha Ballard was the respected postmistress and had held the responsibility for the Ravens Hollow mail. She arrived in the Hollow with her daughter, Queenie, after the Gold Rush was slowing down, after a tragedy that had caused the death of the girl's father and her two siblings. The Born and Bred took the pair to their hearts, after listening to their sad tale. And who could resist Queenie's chubby face with her warm smile? Queenie was only a baby when it happened, so had no recollection of the tragedy. Bertha would never confirm or deny the stories that floated around from time to time.

Queenie felt the stories belonged to someone else and became completely detached. The mystery of the fire was alien to her. That did not belong in her world. It was thought Fred Ballard had started the fire after an argument with Bertha. The rumour-mongers never gained any ground with their surmising. The postmistress became more respected for her strength and persistence to achieve a good life for herself and Queenie. Their love and devotion for each other was so strong. Many envied the relationship.

It was a still, cloudless night. All the young ones were enjoying the Easter carnival, with the hayride heading out to one of the larger sheep properties where the barn dance was to be held in the shearing shed. The air was full of excitement. Tom had asked Queenie to go with him. They had watched each other grow up. Queenie had never thought

Tom would be interested in her and was a little surprised when he asked her to go with him to one of the most important social events the Hollow had.

The stars lit their smiling faces as Tom helped Queenie down from the wagon, picking hay from her dress. Jack, the fiddle player, made musical magic and the fun began. Queenie felt the thrill of the night. As Tom dropped her home, he had decided she was going to be his life's partner.

Queenie fell in love with ease. Her world had only known love. Tom became another dimension and his aura provided her with fulfilment. The children came along quickly—a girl for Queenie and a boy for Tom. Their life and love were perfect.

The children were teenagers when Tom was shot through the heart and died without a moment of pain. It was a robbery at the Golden Nugget, his birthplace, his true home, now the place of his demise.

Tom watched as the black ravens gathered, circling above him, their soft feathered wings flapping. He felt their strength lifting him high into the sky. Tom watched his world disappear. Among the birds, he saw the face of a small oriental gentleman waving to him. Tears were running from his sightless eyes.

A monument was erected in the corner of the park. Tom would be honoured and acclaimed for his bravery and the service he had provided for the community.

Queenie had lost her mother only two months before Tom. A haze covered her days, talking to her mother as if she was still in the room with her. And Tom was her constant companion. Her love kept them together in death as in life.

Queenie knew Tom junior would join the force. She would hear Tom's voice countless times, telling her it was in his blood. Tom would say, 'Let the boy follow his dreams.' Queenie could never argue with Tom, so that was the way it would be.

The happiest day of Queenie's life was the day Tom called her to come to him. She melted into his arms and they became one.

Descendants from Tom Barlow would hear his voice summon them to their vocation. They would embrace Tom's direction as their true calling. Tom watched over them with great diligence. They were in his care for the time they would be there for the protection of others. There would always be a sergeant Barlow in Ravens Hollow.

Lee Ping had his son. The pride he felt was pure joy; the sadness he felt, the horror of reality. From time to time Lee remembered he had had another son far, far away.

7

THE NEW SMITHS AND
THE NEW HARTNELLS

Dirk and Mary seemed to leave the past behind. There were times, though, Dirk heard his father's voice. His father had died not long after Elva. She would have been pleased he never had time to rebuild his precious church. Dirk would dismiss him. When The Preacher got a chance to get a word through, he was best forgotten. Mary missed her mother at times, but never her father. She knew he had a dark side. Sometimes she felt it creeping into her. Thinking there was no blood connection, she was relieved.

After the birth of her two boys, she convinced Dirk to help her create a small weekly newspaper, letting the locals know who was doing what, and notices of formal meetings important events, births, deaths and funerals. It was slow to take off, but Mary loved looking for interesting stories and spreading the news, even if most knew about it all before it was in print. They called the paper *The Gold Miner*. It became a tremendous success in time. Their sons, Alfred and Harold, would eventually take it over. The articles became more sophisticated, taking in a broader area. The reputation of *The Gold Miner* would grow into a recognised tabloid.

Karl also became a fine citizen, marrying a girl from a wealthy sheep grazing property and adapted to farming well. He eventually took over the large acreage. Karl and his wife, June, also had two sons. Ben would take after his father and go on to work with Karl. John would be a clone of Gustav Schmidt and bring shame on the new Smiths. They all worked hard to erase his misdemeanours from the image they were now projecting.

John was wild from the day he was born. He had mood swings and tantrums that were hard to control, so spent the majority of his childhood locked in his room. Karl and June had no control over their second son. John left the farm and became a roustabout in town, earning enough to look after himself and enjoy the life he was made for—causing trouble and having fun. He would leave four Smith kids around the town from two broken-hearted women. Finally, he left the Hollow. The women, the kids, Karl, June and Ben, never heard from him again. Colin, Will, Matt, and Harry Smith would never know their father or realise they were all clones of Gustav Schmidt whom they never knew a thing about.

The Smiths would always be known by their good looks and high cheek bones. Somehow the line, 'Tell me you love me and I will give you what you want,' would appear from nowhere. It shocked the boys when they said it, not knowing why they had, but it worked most of the time, so they never thought about where it came from.

The Hartnells multiplied.

Billy, Bertie, Dougie, followed in their father's footsteps like he was directing every move, not caring who they hurt along the way. Billy's kids (Jim's kids) Marlene, Patrick, and Morrie grew up on the streets. They did all manner of petty crimes and were arrested from time to time. Their fate was sealed. They would be no-hopers until the end. Marlene missed Jim. He made her feel special. Her mother never gave her much except all her bad habits. Her love for men came in handy when she needed a few bob. Marlene always had that side of the street to fall back on. She always had more money than her brothers. Thankfully she never had any children, leaving that to the boys.

Little Jimmy looked after the lot, trying to pick up the pieces, trying to keep the family together. He was the only one that didn't leave a string of offspring all over town. He worked hard to get some respect from the local folk, so his mother's life hadn't been a complete waste. Jim's blood was embedded in the Hartnell genes. The odd few filtered through with Raylene's did little good. The Hartnells were all dumb bastards.

A ray of light turned to darkness.

Nell came out of nowhere. She was the tiniest woman the locals had ever seen. They called her Fairy. She wore her grey hair flowing down her back, almost touching the floor. Some days, she would weave a purple ribbon through it like a vine. When she smiled, she revealed two gold front teeth. They all wondered if she got them because she owned the Golden Nugget, or she had bought the Nugget because of her gold teeth.

Nell ran the pub with precision, treating everyone with respect—staff and patrons alike. Her charm was intoxicating, just like the alcohol she sold. It wasn't long before everyone loved her. The non-drinkers would come in for a lemonade just to watch her flitting around, working as hard as the staff. She moved so fast some days that the watchers almost expected her to grow wings and fly, just like a fairy.

Fairy Nell never let anyone leave hungry. If she knew they were short of cash, they would get a meal and a box full of goodies to take home for their family.

She wouldn't suffer fools. There were no handouts for the idiots. It was all about fair play and she was disciplined enough to be true to her rules and convictions. Nell had made the Hollow a better place for a short time in its history.

The wrongs that never became right.

Morrie was the worst of Shelia's kids. Whoever the father was, Jim or Billy, it didn't matter. He couldn't be good or bad. His crimes were never smart enough not to get caught. He got locked up more than the others ever did. Sometimes they made him take the blame and laughed as he was hauled to jail. He was a drunken, dumb bastard who had had enough of his life and didn't care about anyone or anything. He wanted out.

Tonight, the Nugget was full to overflowing. Every space inside was taken. Drinkers were spread all over the footpath, even onto the road. Nell couldn't wait to count the takings. It would almost finish off her loan. She danced with joy at her success. Waltzing, smiling, her gold teeth glowing in the dim light as she headed down to the end corner of the back room that was always full of Hartnells and Smiths, to tell them it was time to close up.

She gently placed a hand on Morrie's shoulder. He jumped, swung around, and stabbed a double-bladed knife into Nell's jugular vein. Silence fell over the crowd as if they all had a knife sticking out of their chests. Their hearts broke. The pool of deep red blood framed Nell's petite face lying on the floor of the Nugget, almost in the same place Tom Barlow lay years before. Nell's dark eyes stared at the ceiling, like a surreal sculpture made of stone. Morrie was dragged outside, getting kicked by the angry crowd. The Sentinels moved in quickly, squawking, swooping, pecking at his head and face until he was unrecognisable. Morrie Hartnell was taken to Melbourne and hanged.

Even the hardest of the Hollows' community cried for Nell the day they laid her to rest. A rainbow embraced the whole town as they lowered the coffin into the damp earth. For years to come, every time a rainbow engulfed the town it was called a Fairy Day.

Lee Ping welcomed Nell. He had watched the enchantment she had spread in the time she had spent in the Hollow. She didn't deserve to be left behind, but she had been deprived of the opportunity to fulfil her life's plan. Therefore, she faced eternity in limbo with Lee Ping's community of lost souls. Morrie would make his way to Raylene's side, not sure whether he was her grandchild, or she would have been his stepmother of sorts. Whatever the relationship was, she didn't care. She didn't really need him with her. Morrie would remain unwanted wherever his life or death took him. Morrie's eyes penetrated into Raylene just as Jim's had. She asked, 'Why, why, why, did she have to endure this Hartnell curse, even in death?'

Mary and Dirk tried to keep as much of the story out of The Gold Miner as they could. They had to protect the town, and some of the Hartnells were their friends. All the kids played together.

They were Born and Bred. Protection was their right. Time would fade the bad memory of Morrie. There would be many more Hartnell and Smith stories to take its place.

8

THE ETERNAL VORTEX

Time circled; moved on. Though time stood still, everything changed. Though everything changed, everything stayed the same.

Australia grew in knowledge, wealth and population.

Lee Ping's lost souls filled the empty tunnels and mine shafts the rapists had left behind after they had stripped the land of all the gold.

Some of the vultures left rich, some poor, some dead, and the souls left behind gathered.

Elva cried. Raylene asked why. They took turns to cuddle the dark-eyed, crying baby. Brenden prayed for forgiveness and dreamed of a girl with pale blue eyes like a stagnant pond. There were always the loud groans from Martha that covered Violet's gentle sobbing. Tom tried to help, but failed. There was nothing left. His spirit was depleted. Dougie cowered in the corner. Fairy danced in front of him, so he never forgot his unspeakable crime. Sometimes he was sure she had fairy wings.

The Born and Bred listened from above. They never spoke of the noises they heard; never told the secrets of Ravens Hollow. All was hidden behind closed doors. The Hollow looked like an ideal pioneering town left behind in a time capsule.

The Smiths and the Hartnells split into good and bad. The bad made it very hard for the good to thrive, but they did, with the hope to eventually prove their worth. The bad knew how to recruit their numbers. They would pick the weakest of a new litter and it wasn't long before a new batch of young hooligans were on board for all the harassments they could muster up. The bad filled every dark corner of the Hollow. The ones that knew stayed as far away as they could.

Mary and Dirk gathered the good Smiths and little Jimmy, the good Hartnells, and worked on building a new reputation for their families. So, the journey began to build a workable community, without letting the Hollow's secrets be known to the outside world.

All the British-ruled states came together and Federation was born. Australia came of age with its own government and Prime Minister. With strength, hope and pride, the population marched into the new century.

And the Vortex became deeper, darker, gathering the dead that were not accepted into a peaceful resting place.

9

ROBERT HAMISH MACKENZIE

When hope fades, hope rises again.

Robert, a strong-willed, handsome young man, couldn't abide by the rules of his Scottish heritage, to the shame of his family, resulting in expulsion. He abused his rich, socially privileged life by his inability to take any responsibility to make his mother and father proud. They had given up hope of him ever amounting to anything but a lazy drunk if they didn't come up with a plan.

Robert Hamish MacKenzie was to be sent to the colonies. He was to be given land in a Central Victorian town with an annuity for five years until he was established well enough to look after himself. The only advice his father gave him was to find a decent woman to make his wife and he might become a respectable member of society with some merit.

He left under a cloud of disgust from his family and people he thought were his friends. He decided he would make the most of not being under watchful, restrictive eyes and make a new life he had control over.

The long voyage gave him time to scan the ship for the prettiest girl to court and make his wife before they reached the Australian shores. The captain married Robert and Jane with the approval of Mr and Mrs Cameron. The father lived up to the origin of the Cameron nickname, which was 'big nose'. Robert hoped his children didn't inherit it and took after the beauty of their mother. Her silky blonde hair fell down past her shoulders. Her peaches and cream complexion and blushing pink cheeks complimented her large, innocent eyes. Jane left her parents for the first time in her life. She would never see them again. An occasional letter would be the only connection, as her parents were to stay in Sydney.

The newly wedded couple set off on a new adventure, heading for Melbourne. They were strangers. Robert was much older than Jane and she felt she was replacing her missing father with Robert. Jane hoped she would become fond of him in time. She really had no feelings for him at all. She thought her parents had her best interests at heart, so would do her best to face what lay ahead with a conviction to honouring those who cared for her. Robert and Jane had no idea where they were going—only to a mining town in Central Victoria.

The journey was arduous. The condition of the land was rough, with huge granite boulders covering the ground as far as the eye could see. Robert could see the look of disapproval on Jane's face as they endured the ride. The bleak countryside was dry and dusty. She was sure the land had not had the pleasure of rain for some time. She was missing the green Scottish landscape already. The town his father had chosen for his rebellious son was almost depleted of gold and was attracting rich graziers. 'That is where the money is,' his father had said.

Robert began to think his punishment was going to be greater than he was equipped to handle. They had to walk a mile to the block of land from the train station and were exhausted by the time they stood in front of the empty expanse of rocky dirt that was their property. Jane was on the verge of tears. Robert was speechless.

The ravens circling over their heads distracted them from their disappointment. They seemed to be trying to tell them something. Of course, they had no idea what, but somehow, they felt a sudden positivity. They would make plans. They would have to stay at the Golden Nugget Hotel until they could clear the land and get some sort of dwelling erected.

Robert employed local builders and roustabouts to help with the building. It was his first encounter with the Smiths and Hartnells. A little shocked, he learned what this outback country was all about and what hardships he would have to face. Jane had no choice but to agree with everything Robert wanted. And that's how it was. She supported him from day one and tried to hide the disappointment of being stuck in this dirty, old, scary place called Ravens Hollow.

The buildings of the Hollow, with their worn timber, rusted iron roofs and fences, looked prehistoric to Jane after living in Edinburgh, a modern city, all her young life. She was finding it hard to bear. The only comfort was her music box, with her Gaelic songs she would play to remind her of home. Robert told her very little of his past. His persona told her he had come from an upper-class family, which gave her confidence she would be looked after.

She followed his every footstep, helping where she could in the dirt and rubble, clearing and lifting rocks. Her soft, pink hands became rough with the dirt ground in. She felt worn and tired, like the buildings that surrounded her. It seemed the only piece of land that had been left, because no one wanted to have to build into the rock. The task was more arduous because of the steep slope. Laughing, Robert had said, 'Maybe we should be looking for gold instead of building a store and dwelling.' Jane laughed along with him, really wanting to cry. Eventually, there was a general store that only had a dirt floor, as did the two small, dark and dingy rooms at the rear. The floor would harden and shine with time. Jane would have to be content with the small rooms until the second story could be built.

Another hardship Jane would endure: the rooms having no natural light, being built into the rock. Robert told her the solid rock base was a foundation that would last forever. Jane didn't want to be there forever. Depression was becoming her companion.

Jane tried to be happy making a home for them in the two rooms. The only way out was through the front door of the shop, making the track around to the back where Robert had erected a lean-to and a privy, a daily and nightly chore. 'One day I will build you a home on the top with a large veranda where you can sit and watch the goings on in the street below and a back door that will take you out to the yard.' Jane would wait.

The store did well. Robert's father was right again. Jane got her veranda and watched the world go by. The same people passed by at the same time every day. The horses were pulling stylish buggies, but more and more modern cars were chugging along Goldsmith Way, the main road in and out of town. The main street veered off to the left, where The Nugget and most of the original businesses were.

The MacKenzie General Store now took over the two back rooms that had been their home and extended out to the side. The large corner block allowed a large storage-shed to be built. It was entered off Mill Street where the stock was delivered. A side gate with a narrow path led to the back door to enter the top level. Her home over the store was Jane's pride and joy. It had strong blue stone foundations, solid red brick walls, and her veranda.

The timing of the birth of their first son, James, and then, within the appropriate time, the second son, Hamish, all within the five-year guideline worked well. Robert became his own man and took great pride that he was respected, and in time, became a community leader. He promoted new living standards for the betterment of the community.

Life was harmonious. Robert was happy with the store, and Jane happy with the children. They both felt they had been successful in their own way and had put Scotland out of their minds.

The boys were reaching manhood the day Jane woke to find Robert lying beside her.

He was usually up and about before her, and most days had the fire in the bedroom stoked, warming the room before she had to get the boys' breakfast. She became nervous. The room was cold and she could see the black birds sitting on the balcony railing through the glass doors.

Jane froze. Robert was dead. It was some time before she moved downstairs to get help. She wasn't sure how she should feel about the loss of her husband. They had grown together in some ways, though Jane never felt they belonged to each other. She would grieve for this man that had given her the only thing she really cared about—her sons.

The verdict was Robert was just worn out. The high-spirited life he had lived in his youth, the work he had put into his family business and the development of Ravens Hollow had taken its toll. Robert deserved his rest.

After Robert's death, Jane coped well and went about her days as before. She hadn't relied on him a great deal. It was the boys that gave her a reason to live.

War broke out in Europe—the first world war. James decided to fight for the mother land and enlisted. Jane didn't approve of his selfishness. How could he leave me too?

Hamish was going to take over the store and move into his father's shoes. Jane watched the world go by from her veranda—the same people, the same time every day. She watched the blow-ins come and watched them leave. Some stayed longer than others.

She wondered if it was the unexplained sounds that drifted through the streets from time to time—the church bell ringing for no reason, the baby crying from Mabel Burns cottage when there was no one living there, the cries, the screams on dark nights, that made them move on. And there was always the Ravens.

She watched the seasons come and go and the changing colours. In the winter, most of the trees lost their leaves, but not the flowering gums Robert had the foresight to have planted up both sides of her street. When there was a breeze, the perfume reached the veranda. The eucalyptus fragrance overcame the odours from the dirt and grime the Hollow produced on a daily basis. She wrote letters to

James every day and prayed for his safe return, trying to be positive about the situation that threatened the world.

Hamish was out most nights, telling his mother he was in love and was thinking of marriage. Jane wondered why he had never brought the girl home to meet her. Her loneliness grew. She sat on her veranda long after dark in her rocking chair that Robert had bought for her one day when the building had been finished. Her heart softened that day. The fondness was building between them.

She dreamed of Scotland. Jane thought she had been happy with her life, but now she wasn't sure. Why had her parents brought her here all those years ago? She never questioned anything. She just existed, breathing in and out.

James was killed at Gallipoli. The day Jane received a letter from his captain was the beginning of the end for her. The captain had sent all the letters she had written back to her. James had saved every one of them on his person. She opened them, hoping for a reply. There was none. The dried eucalyptus leaves she had enclosed to remind him of home drifted slowly to the floor.

A week later, Hamish decided to bring home his girlfriend. Jane tried to be polite. She wanted to like the girl. Her name was Betty from out of town, well out of town.

Betty was black. What more can this country do to me she thought? This last thing she could not accept. When they had gone, she lit a lamp to go to the privy, negotiating the rough path, stumbling in her sadness. When shining the light inside the door, she saw there were maggots crawling all over the wooden planks that formed the seat over the can. She turned, lifting her long skirt and squatted on the ground, losing the last little piece of dignity she had managed to hang on to in this primitive place she was forced to call home.

Jane went to her veranda and settled into her rocking chair with her music box and played the music from the home of her birth as loud as she could and died of a broken heart. The black birds circled with sadness.

HAMISH AND BETTY MACKENZIE

Love comes with courage and madness.

After Hamish and Betty married, Betty was sure it was Jane, this petite, pretty woman with a bonnet tied with a blue ribbon under her chin, standing in the corner of the veranda. That was the beginning of Betty's madness. In the echoing distance, bagpipes penetrated her mind. The MacKenzie general store started to lose customers as soon as Hamish and Betty were married and Betty moved into the home Jane had created.

Nothing was changed for Hamish. It was like having a replacement for his mother with the comforts of company in his bed. They were happy until they realised it was Betty's black skin and her culture the customers didn't like. It had brought some of her people to the store, in turn keeping more white locals away. Hamish loved Betty and there was no way he was going to give in to the bigotry.

He had learned to enjoy Betty's mob and spent time at their campfires learning their DajDaj Wurrung language; almost becoming one of them. He had hoped Betty would have been accepted by his people in the same way. It was not to be.

A year later, the locals began to return to the store out of necessity. Hamish had his father's charm. He worked hard and the business came back to being better than ever. Betty stayed hidden in the house, never going on to the veranda. Isolated from the world, she stopped going to see her mob. They thought she had gone to the other side.

When the children came along, James Robert, a son, Hannah, a daughter, they were white. Their dark, curly hair and dark eyes were the only telltale signs of mixed blood. Betty's mob then turned their backs on her. Altogether losing her closest family, she was white now. She had left their dreaming. Her people didn't want her. James' people didn't want her either. She drifted between, in a void of nowhere.

She loved James Robert. He looked like Hamish. It was different with Hannah. She looked so much like Jane she scared her. Betty would catch Hannah staring at her with a judging eye. She was sure Jane was there telling her she should go back to her own side of town. Betty was going mad, hearing voices from her elders, fearing the curse of them pointing the bone; Jane telling her to get away from her son and grandchildren.

Hannah died of diphtheria before her second birthday. James Robert was just three. Betty believed she had failed in every aspect of her life. Darkness surrounded her. Hamish tried to convince her it wasn't her fault Hannah died.

Diphtheria was taking a lot of children from their families at this time. That wasn't what Jane was telling her every time she closed her eyes. Jane was saying, 'I have her now, you black bitch. You took my son. Now I have taken your daughter.'

Betty seemed to live in another world where Hamish and James Robert didn't belong. Closing the store after a long day, Hamish climbed the stairs into the house, looking forward to dinner and an early night. He was sure Betty would get over her grief before long. He did spend as much time as he could trying to support her. He thought to himself, *I am too tired tonight for Betty's sadness, just too tired.*

When he reached the top of the stairs, he could see James Robert playing on the living room floor with his toy soldiers. 'Where is mummy?' Hamish asked, wondering why there was nothing happening in the kitchen. The boy shrugged his shoulders. Hamish lit a lamp and headed out to the back of the house. He worried. This wasn't like Betty. She would have taken a light with her.

The path out to the privy was rough and overgrown. He called. There was no answer. Maybe she had gone out onto the street looking for something. He went out through the side gate. She was nowhere to be seen. Turning to go back into the house, the light from his lamp caught her through the half-closed door of the wash house that housed a trough and copper. Hamish held his breath as he opened the door.

Betty was hanging from a rope slung over a beam. She must have been there for some time. A purple face was shining through her black skin, and for some reason, he also remembered the ashes that were still glowing under the copper. The sight would live with Hamish for the rest of his life. There wasn't enough time to save Betty from her madness. James Robert never remembered a thing about his mother. His father told him very little. Life went on.

Betty joined Lee Ping and watched from afar. She had found a place to belong, a comfortable home where there was no judgement. She cried, 'I am a free moo-roan (spirit).'

Light crept into her darkness as she watched James Robert grow into a fine young man by his father's side. He eventually married Dottie Barns from across the street. Her parents owned the ironmongers. Betty was pleased with the match. She would finally be forgotten and her black skin wouldn't bring shame on the MacKenzies ever again.

The Born and Bred kept the secrets hidden away. Anything that was detrimental to Ravens Hollow was never mentioned, true to their code of silence[1].

---

[1] DajDaj Wurrung REF. Language of central Victoria by John Tully

10

DR MARION UNA MACKENZIE

The length of a life is the shortness of time.

Marion felt a sharp pain that reminded her of her pending demise. A two-hour drive was hard for her these days. Why was the disease spreading so quickly? She had hoped for more time. She was the one that saw a cancer patient at the beginning, and more than often, at the end. Her knowledge was playing tricks on her and this disease was not playing the game to her rules. She wasn't finished with this life yet. There were many loose ends that had to be put to rest first.

Marion hadn't been back to Ravens Hollow for fifty years. She never thought the day she left that she would ever be travelling this road again. She didn't want to return to the town of her birth or to the old haunting memories. Marion had had a successful life. She had followed her dreams, although the plans she had made with David were not to be, she had to make it on her own in her own way.

It had been so hard in the beginning. There had been many struggles to face in the early days; everything she had planned was destroyed in one moment, a moment she had buried deep in her mind until today as she travelled back to her past. She had refused her father's request to come back for her mother's funeral. The hurt was still too deep. Her father's solicitor had contacted her sometime after her father, James Robert MacKenzie's, death asking what she wanted to do with the property. It was quite valuable and he would arrange for it to be put on the market and sold. It meant she would have to go back, so the instructions were for him to find tenants and she would take care of it later. Now it was later, fifty years later.

The house was deserted. Tenants never stayed long—blow in and blow out. That was the way in the Hollow. How was she going to set foot in it again? Why didn't she tell the solicitor to get rid of it? Why not forget about the child? She should have ignored the nagging feeling the child deserved to choose whether she wanted to be in this place that was rightfully hers. There was no one else.

The solicitor was going to organise the things she would need in the place for her comfort for the week or so of her stay. She would take care of all the legal arrangements and be back in Melbourne before she needed palliative care. She was well-respected by her peers and always made an impression on every patient that came through her door. The MacKenzie charm, along with her kind nature, made Marion easy to love.

Marion had arranged all her needs with her colleagues. They had their instructions. Her network would be there, if only this disease would play the game. She had the past to get rid of. It was time. It would be a simple process—legal papers to be signed, arrange any major repairs, get help to clear out any rubbish that had been left behind. She had sold her practice along with her Toorak town house that had been her home for thirty years.

Tied up with her own everyday activities and city life, she had never thought of the countryside or the people that were primary producers and the life she had experienced as a child. Marion was taken by surprise, seeing the land devoid of colour. The grass had gone. Only grey dirt and dust remained. Brown leaves were falling to the ground, blown away by a gentle breeze. The cloudless sky, with the rays of sun streaming through the dying trees, gave her an eerie feeling of being in a desert. She wondered whether she was on the right road and pulled over to gather her thoughts. Apprehension and doubts surrounded her. She was heading into the unknown.

Marion had not expected the years of drought to have had such an effect on the land. It was unrecognisable 'Why did I imagine it would be the same?' she thought to herself. In fifty years, everything must have changed. Marion had hoped the Hollow had changed over the time; that no one would remember her, and she wouldn't remember the trauma, opening old wounds that had never healed. How could they? There was always the child in the back of her mind.

Kilometres away of the city now, and there were flashes of an old fence, a tree or farmhouse, rusty tin sheds that were taking her back, back to another time, one she didn't want to revisit. Marion had no choice. She would have to square her shoulders and make good use of the time left for her.

Sorrow surrounded her. Seeing the land deteriorating before her eyes was making the drive harder than she thought—the usually white sheep with their wool blackened with dry dirt and the cattle with every rib exposed. She knew this was not going to be easy. She hadn't reached the town where she thought she would face her grief. Why was this land she had never thought of for fifty years tugging at her heart?

The sudden arrival of the Sentinels surprised her. She had forgotten. How could she, after the farewell they had given her when the bus she was escaping in sped out of town? This time was different. They were loud and violent when she left. Now they circled overhead, softly swooping one at a time, their soft mellow sounds like music. They waltzed around her car. They weren't ravens; they were ballerinas. She watched their shadows on the road ahead. Their ballet was leading her home.

She passed the tree they spent so many summer days sitting, dreaming and sheltered under when they got caught in the rain. It was the only green to be seen. Tears filled her eyes. She had put David out of her mind many years ago. She prayed he wasn't the Hollows doctor, as was his family's tradition. Could the Sentinels read her mind? Her emotions were like a knife's edge, cutting into her, making her bleed. She had to get control. This place and the memories were taking her back to places she didn't want to go.

Marion passed the storm water drain that ran under the length of the town. She had read in the Melbourne Sun one morning a few years ago how twins had been drowned and a giant grid had been placed over the entrances, as the kids had used it as a shortcut from one end of town to the other when there was no rain.

The knife went through her again. She knew from the names in the report there was every chance the twins would have been related to the child. She couldn't cope with that now; it was not the time to think about what happen in the drain.

Fearfully, she drove on, reaching Ravens Hollow just before dusk. The solicitor was to leave the key under the back door mat, which she thought was strange in the current time, considering the rising crime rate. As she passed Mabel Burns Cottage, she stopped, surprised to see a figure picking flowers in the front garden, a scene she remembered. Could it be Jessica?

Marion was heading into a time warp. Her mind was foggy from the long drive. 'That must be it,' she thought. 'I just need to rest so I can get on with the job.' That was the way she had got through the last fifty years— focus and get the job done. By the time she put the key in the back door of her childhood home, she had relived her friendship with Jessica.

After the second world war Gloria Gordon, with her daughter, had moved to the Hollow looking to get away from the city. The bewilderment of grief was suffocating Gloria.

Alf Gordon had signed up and joined the army when the second world war started. Jessica was just a baby when he left, so it was just Gloria and Jessica for some time. It was sometime later Alf had a week at home before being sent to New Guinea. That was when the baby was conceived. Gloria was never able to let Alf know he had a son. When the baby died a month after his birth, she couldn't let Alf know he had a son to mourn.

Gloria was absorbed in her own pain and loneliness. Nothing mattered to her anymore. She looked after Jessica in a nonchalant way and was indifferent to her feelings, only looking after both their immediate needs. Gloria was reaching for a lifeline when the opportunity to acquire a cottage in the country became available.

The government was helping to place war widows. Her future was secure on a small pension in a small cottage in the country. She only had a vague recollection of what was going on around her most days. She could hide away for ever. The cottage would be her saviour. Gloria had no recollection of Alf's face. He was lost to her forever.

Vines and blackberries seemed to engulf the small timber structure of Nurse Mabel Burn's cottage. The roof and water tank didn't leak, so that was a bonus. With Jessica's help, Gloria would make the cottage livable. No one had ever stayed in the cottage for longer than a week or so. Everyone said it was haunted.

The first time Gloria heard the baby cry, she felt a warmth that had been lost to her since she had lost her baby boy. She felt his presence surrounding her. 'Sam, I am coming, I am coming,' she was whispering around the cottage, running from room to room.

Jessica had to walk past Marion's on her way to school. They took the long walk up the hill together. Jessica confided in Marion about the goings on in the cottage. She thought her mother was going mad, always saying, 'Your baby brother is crying. I must go and feed him,' and off she'd go looking for him.

In time, Jessica noticed her mother seemed happier than she had ever seen her before, so accepted the way things were. Jessica heard stories about Mabel Burns and the baby crying. Gloria wasn't interested in gossip. It was her baby, Sam, and she would be there for him when needed. They settled down into a peaceful life, the three of them.

Jessica and Marion shared the walk and little secrets on the way to school every day. They met Jenny who lived in the schoolhouse with her mother and aunty, Aunty Bert, Jenny called her.

Roberta Stewart was a teacher at the growing Hollow school. The three girls were great friends, always together giggling and telling secrets, having afternoon tea and playing cards with Marion's mum, Dottie, after school.

Marion smiled as she walked through the door with an intrepid step, remembering Jessica and Jenny, her school friends that she shared so much with. She might find time to see if that was Jessica who had come back to the haunted cottage. She gave a little chuckle.

The house was much as she left it so long ago. She couldn't bear to go into all the rooms now. She found the solicitor had left an Esky with milk and coffee on the bench and had the power connected. There was a new kettle on the stove. Having made her coffee, she sat on the one comfortable chair that had been provided in the living room. Memories came flooding back to her. How was she going to face this time? Her strength was failing.

As Marion laid her head down on the single bed that had been made up in one of the smaller rooms, she heard a familiar sound, 'BORINE, BORINE' (darkness) over and over coming in waves. She was a child again, falling asleep listening to the sounds of the house, never knowing what the sounds were, or what they were trying to tell her.

She woke with a start.

'Is there someone there?' she called nervously. There was no answer. Feeling it was her mother. She didn't know why. Feelings for her mother were lost the day she told her to leave; Dottie said she couldn't take any more disgrace from this family. Marion knew she had a right to be ashamed of her but wasn't sure what else there was to be ashamed of. She was to hurt to care about anything else but her own problem, and she had expected a mother to stand by her, not send her away.

They had been great friends. She had loved her mother. They would laugh and swap stories about all the goings on in the town. One day when Marion was about twelve, she came home to find her mother in bed, her head under the covers and she wouldn't talk. She didn't even lift her head when Marion came into the room. Her father would get the meals. Marion would take them in and try to talk about her day. Her mother never responded. She had lost the mother she had loved and needed.

That's how it was. Marion can remember the day she got such a fright when she saw blood running down her leg. She ran into her mother's room, thinking she was dying and wanted help. Dottie looked at her as if she were a stranger and said, 'Go and get the small towels from the cupboard. Get some pins and make sure you wash the towels all the time. Don't be dirty and be careful. Years later, when she needed her help again, she said, 'Just like your father. Get out!' So why was she feeling her nearness now?

Marion was unsure what was happening with the blood thing and shared her dilemma with her friends. Neither had had the experience. Jenny suggested they go to her mother, Claudia, and Aunty Bert and ask them for help.

That was Marion's first real visit to the schoolhouse. The adults were both there and were only too willing to help with all the ins and out of the female anatomy, scaring the girls somewhat. Thankfully, Marion knew she would live. Every woman has to have the curse. The girls would spend hours with Claudia and Roberta after that day.

When you stepped inside Jenny's home, it was like going into a different world. Claudia kept house, while Bert went to work. She was a dedicated teacher, always happy, singing, laughing, and Jenny's mother, the dedicated home maker. Marion felt as if she was walking into a dolls' house, frilly and pink, smelling of lavender. Claudia's favourite music drifted through every room. It was like a fairy tale existence. The locals became envious of their happiness.

Marion couldn't think any more about her school friends for now. She had to get to the solicitor. She descended the stairs that took her into the shop. It was musty and damp. The shelves had a few left-over packets of old oats, flour, tea and things like that. 'Why hadn't the rats and mice eaten them?' she wondered.

Opening the door to the street, she couldn't believe her eyes. There they were, the two of them. She recognised them straight away. There was no mistake, sitting on the seat outside the undertakers. She almost laughed. *Wish they were booking in*, she thought. If only she could be here for that—she might see some justice.

Did they know she was back? Bile rose into her mouth. She almost turned around. Even if they didn't recognise her, they would guess it was her. Who else would be coming out of the shop that had been deserted for so many years? She wanted to go back inside and hide away like she had for the last fifty years.

Somehow Marion made it to Main Street, into the office for the appointment with Mr Parker the son of her father's original solicitor. The instructions had been left there, so the old files had been pulled out of their archives. All was straightforward. The property was Marion's to do with as she pleased.

Mr Parker found a key in the file with a note saying it was for her to open her father's desk that was left in one of the back rooms of the shop. Marion thanked Chas Parker for his help setting the house up for her and gave him some instructions regarding the child.

Marion struggled back to the house. They had gone from the seat over the road. She was relieved by the time she reached the top of the stairs. She was exhausted. needing to make a coffee and sit down. The kitchen was much the same as it was the day she had left. Her father had upgraded it when the Hollow eventually got the power connected, long after most of Victoria had been enjoying the modern convenience.

She remembered the celebrations and the Switch on Ball held in the community hall. Her mother had dressed her up for the occasion and all the kids had a great time. They had never been out of bed so late. It seemed like a million years ago now. Not daring to go out onto the veranda at this time in case they returned. She had often sat and watched people sitting on the seat waiting to go into see the Mr Walton the Undertaker. Wondering why they had been sitting there. They must know she was back. Her mind was in turmoil. She wanted to escape this place. She didn't want to belong here.

Marion fell asleep to her sounds—BOONDYIL (wisdom knowledge) over and over. She slept until late afternoon. She remembered she hadn't needed any pain medication since she had been in the house. Her mother's presence drifted over her again. Her mind was swimming with confusion. Maybe she would wander down to the south end of town, to Mabel Burn's cottage and see if it was Jessica there in the garden picking flowers.

It was nearly spring, but the drought was hiding that fact. She had noticed the garden at Mabel Burn's cottage had been kept alive and was thriving. Gloria always had it that way. The key and the desk will be for another day. She couldn't take anymore. What would she need to know after all these years? Nothing would take away her mother's last words: 'Get out! I can't take any more shame. You are just like your father.'

To Marion's knowledge, her father was highly respected and the locals supported the store. Even when others moved in and tried to take some of his business, the older ones said he had the MacKenzie charm. She always felt any problems may have been in their marriage would have come from her mother.

She left the makeshift bedroom. *Funny*, she thought, *this room was never a bedroom.* Her mother used it to store old clothes, books and papers. She was told to stay out. It was only rubbish. It must have been cleared away over the years. She was sure there wouldn't have been any value in the bits and pieces she remembered seeing. Maybe that is why she felt her mother's presence. It was her storeroom. All her secrets hidden away.

Marion laughed to herself. She didn't think her mother was the type to have many secrets. She would clean the cupboard out when she felt up to it.

Marion wandered out to the veranda. Chas Parker had left an old rocking chair there. The flowering gums seemed to have survived the drought, but the street was covered in dust. The deep blue stone gutters were full of dried leaves and other rubble. These sights were so alien to her. She felt as though she had stepped back in time and she didn't have the strength to stop it. She was falling into the past.

The lolly shop looked the same. She was sure that was Beth, sweeping the path as her mother had done before her. The shop next door was empty, with old brown paper covering the windows as it had been the day Marion had left. It couldn't be the same. It had been the doll shop. She didn't want to face that memory now.

11

MARION'S MEMORIES

They are there again today. She could see the remains of the Hartnell red hair was now white and the strong Smith jawline and high cheek bones. Her stomach churned. She couldn't take her eyes away. Memories flashed in front of her.

Thomas came out of the front door of the Undertakers and spoke to them. They all looked up to the veranda and stared as if they were waiting for her to come out through the French doors and perform for them, to wave like the queen of this shitful place, her audience. Maybe that was what her life was—a performance and she was the fallen star.

Rex Hartnell and Leon Smith sat there, the same smirk on their faces as they had the day they watched her leave. Why did she think they would be gone? Their egos would have kept them here, dominating this place. They were an imprint on her brain, like a dark space, like a cancer that had taken fifty years to grow.

Thomas had always been kind to her, even warning her and relaying what they were saying about her. She was surprised he was speaking to them now. Time heals most things, so they say. Why wasn't it working for her? Why was her mind dredging up all this kid stuff that should be gone and forgotten?

THOMAS WALTON

The long shadows hold back the sunshine.

Andrew and Josie Walton arrived in Ravens Hollow in the spring, when the trees were full of flowers and the gardens around the miners' cottages were a multitude of bright colours. The clear cerulean sky lifted Josie's spirits. She felt her unborn child stir in her womb, filling her with hopeful anticipation.

Andrew had finally found the courage to tell his father he wanted to move out and go into his own business. He was tired of the old man looking over his shoulder, picking on every little thing he did.

Andrew had found a parlour advertised in the Melbourne paper. It was just right, a small country town well out of the city, a place where his child could grow and eventually take over from him when the time was right. He would be cautious not to make the same mistakes his father made with him. In their naïvety, they thought it looked so idyllic. How could anything go wrong? They would be accepted because their child would be Born and Bred.

The black birds surrounded them, diving close to their heads. Their sounds were soothing, not like crows at all. They didn't scare Josie. She thought it was odd. She was usually frightened by birds so close.

They lived in a small cottage at the back of the chapel. The work area was on the other side, out of sight, in the front of the building. Facing Goldsmith Way was the office and the interview room. The Waltons made it a very pleasant environment and they seemed to be accepted as a needed commodity for the community. Andrew was his own man. He did his work with pride.

Josie was happy. Thomas, their baby boy, filled her days and Andrew filled her nights. Her simple mind had simple needs. She thought her family was accepted as one of them. The Born and Bred disguised it well. She never realised they weren't. They were never invited to anyone's home and some stopped Thomas from playing with their children.

Marion watched Thomas growing up and took it upon herself to look after him, as he was shunned by the rest of the local kids. Being an Undertaker's son was not something people wanted to think about. He was always telling her he loved her. She would just laugh. What harm could that be? He must have seen her as a sister figure. As a teenager the bad Smiths and Hartnells named him the Terminator, poking at him and saying when someone visited him, 'They never came back,' and shouted at him, 'You are the Terminator,' and roughed him up most days as he walked home from school.

No one seemed to care. Marion tried, but she knew if she was seen to take his side, she would be in the bullies' path and she already knew she was a target. Thomas had told her they said she was up herself and thought she was better than anyone else. One day, they would get her and bring her down so she would know she was no better than them. Marion never thought about it too much. She had her girlfriends, and then there was David.

Marion was at a loss. She wanted to put everything out of her mind. Her mother was still lurking around. She could feel her, smell her. That musty smell of her room—there was never any air. She refused to open the window. She must have bathed when Marion was at school. She realised she had never seen her out of her bed since that day. She wondered if there had been something she should have done for her. Why didn't her father do something? She would never have let one of her patients get into that position. Why didn't David's father do something?

Guilt covered her like a heavy blanket, weighing her down. She was suffocating. Did she have her eyes shut to what went on in her own family? She was too young to understand. If only she could go back in time, maybe things might have been different. She couldn't open the desk today. That would be for another day. Maybe her mother was trying to tell her something. Marion's time was running out. She just wanted to get the papers signed and get out of this place.

Falling asleep to her childhood comforting sounds, Pal-lert Pal-lert (strong). What was the message? Why hadn't she asked someone? Who would have known? She would venture down to Nurse Mabel Burn's cottage in the morning and see Jessica. The thought of going through the tragedy they shared together was a little daunting, even though it was something she couldn't run from. It was always with her.

JESSICA GORDON

Time stands still while there is someone to remember.

Jessica embraced her. She didn't need a second look to recognise her old school friend. 'Come in. I am so happy to see you,' Jessica smiled from ear to ear. They were teenagers again for just a minute, then it was back to reality. 'I didn't think you would still be here,' Marion said, looking around, seeing nothing much had changed.

'I did leave after you had left. Mum was happy, with Sam still crying for his mother. I had to get away. You and Jenny were gone and I needed to work. It was easier in Melbourne. I landed a good position in a bank and I married one of the tellers.' Her voice saddened.

'I have come back to settle the property.' Marion wasn't about to get into the complicated business; she didn't have the strength. My husband and I bought the cottage so Mum could stay and she did until she passed away.

'Did you become a doctor as you planned?'

'Not quite as I planned, but yes, I have had a successful career.' Marion started to relax. It was so easy. It was like they had never parted.

'Did you get married?' Jessica asked.

'No, I nearly did once but something stopped me. I never needed that commitment. I couldn't receive it or give it, for that matter.'

Marion said it was not a priority. It just would have got in the way. If she wanted, or had time for sex, it was always there for the asking. She didn't know what else marriage had to offer.

'Is your husband with you?' Marion asked.

Jessica looked away. 'I had a little boy too. They were both taken from me in a car accident. I stayed in the bank until I retired. That's when I came back here. Funny, the baby's cry comforts me, just as it did for

Mum.' Tears rolled down her cheeks.

Marion's heart cried for her old friend. She had seen too many women lose their children one way or another over the years, something she was glad to have escaped, in a way.

'Have you ever heard from Jenny?' Marion asked, knowing they could not be together without revisiting the day that changed their lives.

'No. But someone told me that she went to live with her mother's sister,' with a slight giggle.

'Funny how we thought Bert was Claudia's sister.'

'We were so young. That was the day we grew up fast.' Marion gazed into the arrogance of a teenager.

They had walked up the hill as usual. It was a sunny November day, nearly at the end of the school year. They had great plans for the school holidays. Marion was happy. She had subjects with David today. That always excited her. They called into the schoolhouse to pick up Jenny. Bert called out, 'You all go ahead. I'll catch up to you later.'

It was a normal day until the headmaster came into their classroom to ask Jenny if she had seen Miss Stewart. She hadn't come in yet. She was never late. Would you take your friends and walk over to see if everything's alright?

It was strange. Usually, you could set your clock by Roberta, her flaming red hair tied in a plait down her back as smart as ever, with a personality that lifted the gloomiest of days. Just like Jenny's mother, always smiling, waltzing to her music, her happiness was infectious. The girls wandered across the school yard, thinking there couldn't be anything wrong. They had seen the pair earlier and everything was fine. They could hear Claudia's music drifting across the yard—Mozart's Requiem, one of her favourites. They could see the lace curtain billowing out of the kitchen window, and the smell of lavender surrounded them as they got closer.

The girls entered the house giggling about how they got out of work for a while, not that they disliked school at all—they just thought they were bucking the system for once. Marion was the top student; Jessica was the top athlete and Jenny was the best musician and singer. They were the "untouchables" as the bad boys would say, every time they walked past them.

Apart from the music, there was no other sound. They called out. There was no answer. Jenny turned off the music. It seemed annoying. There was a bottle and two glasses with the remains of red wine placed neatly on the table. Why would they be drinking in the morning? They weren't big drinkers. Suddenly, things didn't look right. They hung onto each other's hands and went from room to room.

There they were, in Claudia's bed, everything in place, pansies in the vase on the bedside table. Bert's watch guided her through the day lying on a lace doily Claudia had lovingly washed the day before. At first, the girls thought they were asleep. When they went closer, they saw them wrapped in each other's arms. Bert's mouth was covering Claudia's bare breast. They froze.

Jenny let out a squeaky cry, 'They are asleep, aren't they? They are just asleep. Sisters often sleep in the same bed, don't they? Wake up, please wake up!' She started to sob. It seemed as if they stood there for hours, though it was only seconds. It was a horrible dream. Everything went dark. They turned and ran. They were so scared. They had no idea what they had just seen. Instinctively, they knew the two people entwined in a lover's embrace were dead.

There was a crowd of goggling locals, sirens, police cars. David's father came running. Jenny was bundled into a car with a woman they had never seen before.

The police asked questions. They didn't cry. They could hardly speak. They didn't know what to say. The police could see what they saw. What did they know? They were just scared and shocked out of their teenage brains. Marion's father came to get the girls, taking them home. There would be no more giggling. In those few minutes, their childhood was gone. Neither had a mother they could get any comfort from. They only had each other. Marion's mother said she should never have gone to that perverted house. 'Serves you right! You're just like your father.'

The girls found out later a neighbour had spread the gossip about Bert and Claudia's relationship after Claudia had turned him down. He had asked her to have a drink with him at the Nugget some time. When she said, not wanting to upset him in her gentle way, that she wasn't free to do so, he put two and two together and wasn't going to be insulted by such a deviate. The Born and Bred decided to put the episode to rest. And it was never spoken of again.

It would be years before Marion and Jessica would understand what it really meant and why they chose to end their own lives. They worried so much about Jenny and what had happened to her. They missed the time they all spent together. Claudia was the sweetest thing, always making any troubles they were having disappear with her loving smile and kind works, and Bert's strong advice always choosing the right words at the right time. The laughter around the kitchen table, the picnics they packed and sat on the riverbank and how they enjoyed the stories told of their younger days. It was all gone in a flash, as was the girls' youthful innocence; all taken in a flash, but would never be forgotten.

They never saw Jenny again. Their grief was never recognised and help never came. David was the girls' only support. They would huddle together every chance they got to discuss the matters that led to the tragedy. As time went by, Marion and David became closer together and Marion relied on him more than ever. They never excluded Jessica, but she got the message when it was time for her to leave them alone.

Marion was getting exhausted and had to tell Jessica about her illness. Her old friend put her arms around her, wishing she could do something to help. They had shared so much as young people. She felt so helpless now.

'If there's anything I can do, I will be there for you, I promise.' She was surprised at the sound of her voice. It was her young voice. She was going back in time.

'Have you seen David?' Jessica asked, presuming she would have.

Marion froze. She had to collect her thoughts quickly.

'He was devastated when you left without telling him why. I was too.'

'David is here? I thought he would have moved on.' Marion's voice quivered.

'He never married either.'

'I will see him before I leave.' It was time for her to go. She didn't want to tell Jessica why she had left in such a hurry all those years ago. If only she had confided in her, things may have been different.

They exchanged mobile numbers. 'Have you seen David yet?' rang in her ears. Her emotions couldn't take any more today. Marion wandered back to the store, climbing the stairs, falling into bed. BORINE… BORINE (darkness), listening to her comforting sounds.

Roberta and Claudia joined Lee Ping to roam the streets of Ravens Hollow. Mozart's music could be heard blasting out over the school yard and lavender filled the air. On the anniversary of their death, most Born and Bred ignored it. They didn't want to know about such goings on. Blow-ins thought it was the charm of the old school until there were more sounds they couldn't make sense of, making them uncomfortable, causing them to move on.

12

MARION AND DAVID:
FANTASY OF YOUTH

Marion's first encounter with David was when he came into the MacKenzie store with his mother. Marion and David must have been under school age. It was from that day their friendship began. Both their families, being pillars of the community, set them apart. Being born in the same month and having birthday parties together from the first year of school, was the making of a strong bond.

David's mother and Dottie got on well. As they were all Born and Breds, there was an underlying understanding. The Diamonds lived in a different part of the town from the MacKenzies, so the pair rarely walked home together from school; only when Jenny and Jessica had after school activities did Marion take the longer way home with David. It wasn't until Dottie took to her bed that Marion spent more time with him, finding it hard to go home some days.

David couldn't make sense of what had happened. He had liked Dottie and didn't understand how she could do this to her family. His mother was his strength; a rock to lean on in his growing years. He felt Marion needed the same support.

Marion Una MacKenzie and David Anthony Diamond became known as the Mum and Dad of the school, as their initials indicated. It was confirmation of their friendship. They were a popular pair among the good kids.

After Bert and Claudia's deaths, Marion relied on David more and more. They started planning their future and their adventures into the outside world. There was no doubt David would go to university and follow in the footsteps of all the Diamond men before him. Marion had no idea what she would do with her life. Helping her father in the store wasn't going to satisfy her, she was sure of that. They were the smartest ones in the school, taking it in turns to top the class. No one else came near them. They both came under attack from the Smiths and Hartnells from time to time. It was just accepted that the good kids would have to encounter the bad. It was like the bad kids watched for any opportunity when Marion and David were alone.

Poor Thomas Walton copped it all the time. He didn't have any friends. Marion and Jessica took him under their wing when they could see he had had enough.

The day Marion had a bad experience with a Smith left her shaken. When David found her waiting for him in their usual meeting place on the bench just down from the school gate, she was crying. He had never seen her cry, even when the sisters had died. A rush of sadness came over him and he took her in his arms. That's the day the relationship changed.

'What did he do to you?' he asked, trying not to sound angry. Marion told him how Leon Smith had grabbed her from behind and ran his tongue across the back of her neck, saying, 'What dirty things do you do with David?'

David couldn't stop her from crying. He was so mad. He hadn't even kissed her. How dare that bastard denigrate them in this way? He hated those lowlifes.

Marion had decided to follow David and started to show an interest in medicine. She listened more intently to David about his plans. They met more often, always careful to be away from the eyes of the bad ones. Marion began to long for the comfort of David's arms around her and their kisses had progressed to the real thing, well past a kiss on the cheek. The day David said, 'I love you,' Marion thought there would never be a better moment in her life.

They studied together as much as they could. Marion spent time at the Diamond's. Her father didn't close the store until six, giving her plenty of time to get home to help with the evening meal. She was never sure what her mother ate during the day and never really cared. She was totally focused on getting good marks to follow David. It was harder for girls to get into university than boys, but with her grades and a recommendation letter from Dr Diamond, they were sure she would make it. Marion and David were happier than they had ever been in their young lives. They were working towards a goal. It was giving them the strength they would need to face the future and get out of this toxic town.

The night had closed in earlier than usual and she'd left it too late, leaving David's place to get home before dark. David said he would walk home with her. They had almost reached the store when there were footsteps. They didn't worry chatting away with a cuddle and a kiss, when they thought no one was looking. Suddenly, two boys jumped out in front of them and grabbed David around the neck. One threw David to the ground and kicked him in the ribs, yelling. 'You aren't the only one that will get their hands on this stuck-up bitch.'

Marion screamed as loudly as she could. Someone heard the screams and Sergeant Grant Barlow arrived almost before she had a chance to know what happened. Grant called Dr Diamond. Marion told Sergeant Barlow the names of the boys who had assaulted David. The sergeant said he would talk to them both in the morning and take down their statements.

James Robert had heard the screams too. He ran to get Marion. She was trembling when her father helped her up the stairs. Not wanting to eat; just wanting to go to her room. She had to pass her mother's room to get to her own. Marion didn't even look in. knowing her mother wouldn't feel any sympathy for her, or care what had happened to her for that matter.

Marion's room was her sanctuary; no one ever came in. Her mother didn't care and her father respected her privacy. Her room was at the furthest end of the house, off a narrow passage no one else needed to go through. She never invited David or her girlfriends to her secret hideaway. When she was there, she felt she really was untouchable. And no one would even know how many hours she spent in front of the mirror brushing her curly hair, hoping it would go straight.

The next morning, the boys were taken to the courthouse. One had a broken wrist, the other a black eye. Marion knew David had not had a chance to hit them, certainly not that hard anyway. Nothing was said about how they got their injuries. The magistrate sent them to spend some time in the Newtown Home for Delinquent Boys. There would be peace on the streets of the Hollow. The bad ones would quieten down; the good ones felt free for a time. There was no report of the incident in *The Golden Miner*.

David wasn't badly hurt but became bitter and angry, so alien to his nature. Marion was sad to see him suffer in this way. She tried to support him the way he had done for her when the sisters had died. Their bond became stronger and they relied on each other more and more.

They had their plans. It was the last year of school. Every mark was important to Marion, so the year would be full of study and dreams. Dr Diamond loaned them medical books. They would ride out of town on their old bikes, sit under their favourite tree and discuss what they were reading without much understanding of the contents. Their thirst for knowledge was growing almost to the point of excitement. James Robert encouraged the friendship. David was set to have a secure and strong future. He would make an excellent husband for Marion.

On the last day of the exams, Marion's nerves were creating butterflies in her stomach. She knew this would be the start of years of hard work, but she was so full of hope that she gave herself a strong talking to and pulled herself together. That would be her way for the rest of her life—pull yourself together and get the job done. There was a whole world waiting for her and David. Please, not without David. There would be some weeks before all the results were through and they would know if they had a university placement.

They enjoyed their time together without the pressure of study. David was not quite over the assault, still keeping an eye out for a sight of any

Smith or Hartnell. It annoyed him so much that their town could be ruled over by such hooligans, but they were Born and Bred. David and Marion spent hours talking about what their lives would be like away from the constraints of this small town.

It was a hot summer's day. They swam in the river away from the waterholes that most of the teenagers went to, enjoying their secret private places that seemed undiscovered, always being careful not to fall into an old mineshaft abandoned years before when the miners moved on and the gold had gone. They spent lazy afternoons under the shade of their favourite tree, as the brittle grass tickled their legs. They could never imagine their lives would be anything else but full of hope and joy.

They both had passed their exams with flying colours being joint dux of the school. Did anyone expect it wouldn't be so? The letter came confirming Marion had her place as planned and would be off to Melbourne. She would have to tell her father, when the time was right. She was so excited and couldn't wait to tell David. What could go wrong now?

David didn't seem himself when she bounced in, grinning from ear to ear with the news. The first part of their plan was going wrong before they had started their adventure.

David's father had arranged for him to go to Sydney and study under an old friend of his. He insisted he would get off to a better start and benefit his career, mixing with the right people. He could come back to Melbourne after a year or so. Marion's heart sank.

How could she go alone? She had never been to Melbourne. Her father always said he would take her one day, but it never happened. Determination rose. She wasn't about to give up her dreams. She would just have to get on with it and get the job done. She would wait for David as long as she had to.

They decided they would enjoy the time they had left in Ravens Hollow before they would be separated. There would be eight weeks before she had to be in Melbourne. David had ten weeks before he left for Sydney. They spent every minute they could together. Marion had to tell her father. She wondered why he had never asked what the letter from the university was about. They both were playing a waiting game.

David and Marion made new plans about how they would keep in touch. They convinced each other the time would fly. What was a year? They would have a lifetime to be together. Marion headed home to tell James Robert she would be leaving in eight weeks. She was late, so decided to take a shortcut through the drain. It was summer and it hadn't rained for months. It would be safe. Their positivity would soon be shattered.

13

BEHIND CLOSED DOORS:
A HIDDEN UNKNOWN WORLD

They weren't there today. Relief washed over her. Now she could take her coffee out to the rocking chair and enjoy Jane's veranda. Marion had spent many hours watching the passing parade of locals and blow-ins come and go about their business as the other MacKenzie women had done before her. When she was younger, she watched, hoping for the day she would head out along Goldsmith Way to a different world. She smiled to herself. Yes, she had seen that different world, and apart from the dark shadows she had to carry with her from her time in Ravens Hollow, it had been full of good times and satisfaction. She had achieved more in her career than she had expected of herself.

Marion was ahead of her time and the young women doctors looked up to her. There were fleeting moments she had wished she could have shared her success with her father and even her mother, when one of her patients reminded her of Dottie. Her accomplishments had opened the pathways for women to take, making it an easier task to follow their ambitions.

Being back here in this place was zapping away her confidence. That night in the drain was taking over her life again. The feeling of spinning out of control. Knowing she would have to face it again before finding peace of mind, but the disease was making her weaker every day. She had to get out of here.

Beth was there again, sweeping the path as her mother had done before her. She only ever knew Beth from afar. Her mother always said, 'Keep away from her. She has been tainted by the devil.'

Marion never understood what it meant for many years, why poor Beth was out of bounds to everyone except the bad ones or the ones that were nice to her just to get a sweet that she handed out in the hope someone would be her friend.

Finally, Marion had put all the rumours together and was filled with guilt that she had never been able to befriend Beth, when none of it had been her fault.

Susanna Thornton, along with her teenage son Dan, had arrived at the Hollow late in the night and opened the door to the lolly shop the next day, to the locals' amazement. She had brought her own recipes with her and made the lollies at night in the small back rooms that doubled as their home. Dan would help with the packing and display. They were never accepted into the community as Susanna had hoped they would be. Dan didn't fit in too well with the kids his age either, so they had to be content with the chit-chat they made with the customers.

Many from out of town had no bias towards the Thorntons. They couldn't resist the brightly coloured sweet goodies, and Susanna's special recipe of a fudge that was every one's favourite, making her a pretty profit. Susanna became happy with her lot. Her recipes and Dan seemed to be all she needed. She never thought she would want for anything else.

When the baby arrived, the gossip mongers went wild with stories of who the father was. The spy network worked overtime to make sure they knew everyone's business, good and bad. They had the answer to who the father was, but it was too much for them to cope with and was never spoken about again. It was a shame that the Hollow would not be able to live down. Dan had given his mother the greatest gift Susanna could have ever wished for.

Beth became her pride and joy. She was always dressed in a party dress with her hair curled into tight ringlets. Beth had by-passed Dan. The famous fudge recipe became her mother's major priority. Dan left not long after the birth, armed with the fudge recipe to take on the world.

Dottie had watched as this all unfolded. She had grown up a few doors away and after she married James Robert, watched from the veranda. She forbad Marion to have anything to do with Beth. Beth had had two babies before Marion left the Hollow, so she imagined there would have been more. She was sure there would be blood connections to the child.

It is possible Beth never knew who the fathers of her children were and she would never have known her brother was her father. Another secret the Born and Bred would keep quiet about and hide away from any newcomer, all for the town's reputation.

Next to the lolly shop was the doll shop that had the window covered with old newspaper that had yellowed over the years. Marion stared at the window. It couldn't have been the same paper someone had put up after the tragedy that day over fifty years ago. Marion had been in the store the day it happened. She often helped James Robert weight up smaller bags of sugar and flour and packed the shelves.

Gladys Brown had moved into the shop attached to the Golden Nugget, that had been always covered with the lace curtain to hide the ugly profession that had gone on out the back of the empty front room many years before. Everyone seemed to know Gladys had been a prisoner of war and survived the atrocities of the second world war and what she had she endured at the hands of the Japanese in a Singapore camp. She had seen her nursing friends and colleagues tortured and killed.

The locals had presumed she had been in rehabilitation in the years before coming to the Hollow. Gladys was treated with kindness, as was every returned service man or woman that had seen the horrors of war. Ravens Hollow had lost some of their best and they would be remembered. The men and women who served in the world wars had their names printed boldly in gold on the memorial that was erected in the park overlooking the tribute that had been erected for another Hollow hero, Tom Barlow.

Gladys was a little weird and was never accepted as belonging. Most expected her to move on, but did treat her with a smile and a friendly hello. They even bought a doll when they couldn't resist one that caught their eye as they passed by the shop front. Now the lace curtain had gone, the window had life once more.

Marion couldn't stop herself from remembering the stories behind Gladys' miserable life. She made all her dolls on an old treadle sewing machine in the back of the shop. Her living quarters were upstairs. Marion could watch her from the veranda at night, dancing around with one of her dolls. Sometimes Marion was sure she had made a life-sized doll as a dancing partner.

Marion felt sad for her. She must have been so lonely. She had heard whispers about how the locals saw her doing odd things. The kids would watch through the peep hole in the side wall that had been left there from the old days when the brothel owner would charge some deviant to watch the erotic performance going on.

The spy network watched as they saw her fall in love with the butcher. He was a good Smith and very handsome. Having a pretty wife and a couple of kids. He could see what she was up to, coming in all the time asking him stupid questions about the town, about the different cuts of meat, about things that didn't make sense. Every day she would think of something that would bring her into his shop. He wasn't interested. Family coming first. He started to feel sorry for her and softened his attitude, finally becoming a little smitten.

She kept asking him to come over to see her new dolls. Gladys dreamed of the day the butcher would come and make love to her. She had it all planned. She always left her special nightie on the bed for that day. It was early in the morning the day he knocked on her door, hoping no one would see him. She wasn't prepared and was taken by surprise, becoming flustered. This wasn't the way she had planned her special moment.

'No, not like this,' she pleaded, 'I wanted you to come upstairs.' The butcher, Smithy as he was called, didn't hear her.

He had decided to make her dreams come true, saying, 'Tell me you love me and I will give you what you want.' He was sure he had heard somewhere before. Funny, it didn't sound like his voice. They never made it up the stairs. It happened on her sewing table. Gladys heard the boys giggling and making jokes as they watched through the peep hole in the wall.

The butcher left, satisfied he had fulfilled her needs. Gladys cried. There hadn't been any romance, the soft romantic words she had imagined, only the mysterious voice that seemed to have come out of a tunnel. And the boys would spread the story. She was ashamed. She went upstairs and put on her nightie, looked at the clock, walked down the stairs, and walked in front of the nine o'clock bus that went to Newtown at the same time every day.

Marion and her father heard the screams. Gladys was splattered all over the road, just like roadkill. She could have been a kangaroo for all anyone would have cared. Remembering Gladys's story, she felt a sadness come over her. She had learned to control that feeling over the years, having had to attend so many tragedies. Many months later, the locals watched as the pretty wife and two kids saw the butcher being taken away in a straight jacket, screaming in his madness, 'Tell me you love me and I will give you what you want.'

Marion wondered how many more horrors she would have to remember that were concealed in the depths of history and hidden in every crevice of Ravens Hollow. Did she have to revisit every piece of debris left behind before she could put her past to rest?

As Marion left the veranda, she didn't notice the petite woman, her bonnet tied with a blue ribbon, standing in the corner, watching over Goldsmith Way.

Lee Ping welcomed Gladys to the realm of lost souls, where she found peace at last.

There were times when drivers of the nine o'clock bus to Newtown would see a transparent woman in a flowing nightie running across the road in front of the bus.

14

A KEY, A DESK, ANSWERS: UNLOCKING UNSPOKEN WORDS

J hoo-an-dook (long since) Marion heard the voice as she woke to another day of waiting. Turning her head, she saw the light was creeping through the side of the old blind of the storeroom, hitting the key lying on the chair. It was like a spark stabbing her in the eye. She would have to open the desk today. Sure it would be a waste of time. Marion lay there wondering why she had been drawn back to this house? Why was she stuck in this room? Why hadn't Chas put the bed in one of the bedrooms? She hadn't even gone down to her old room. Maybe she would get that out of the way today. Chas would have all the paperwork ready and she could get out of here in the next couple of days.

Marion couldn't sit on the veranda this morning. They were there staring up at the French doors, waiting for her to appear. She wondered if they talked about the night in the drain, or did they have so many other ego building experiences or was that night one of many? She hated them so much. Why was she putting herself through this agony? Wasn't her pain enough punishment for what she was forced to do?

The day was gloomy. The grey sky was low now. It seemed strange to her when she had almost been blinded by the sun when it hit the key an hour or so ago. Apprehensively, she went down the stairs into the store. She could see an image of her father in her mind. It struck her she had never known him as an old man. She felt ashamed she had held so much silent anger towards him. Marion had always looked on him as the perfect father. He was a gentle, caring man, never raising his voice, even to Dottie. She found it hard to see him as the father who let her down when she need help.

The weight of all these memories was becoming hard to bear. She hoped there was a chair at the desk as there had been when James Robert would sit and fill in the leger. Marion helped him sometimes after school when all her homework was done. The back room was dark and damp. An old globe didn't light the room well. A desk and chair were the only things left. The chill in the air was eerie. Marion had an urge to turn around and leave. What would anything her father has to say matter to her now? She was dying. Nothing could be changed. Wondering how she was going to get through the day, she sighed and pull herself together. She would get the job done.

The brass key turned the lock easily. She rolled back the top and stared at the envelope that had sat there for so many years, untouched. Her hands trembled as she held it to her heart. Seeing her father's handwriting had a profound effect on her. This small part of him that had been left behind. She would have to gather all her strength to open the letter.

Dear Marion

It is my hope that one day you get to read this letter. I have made too many mistakes that have affected your life. I am not asking you to forgive me. Maybe the explanation might give you some clarity. I had planned to tell you everything when you were twenty-one. When you left, it didn't seem right to burden you with things that were out of your control. I thought there would be a better time. It never occurred to me that I would never see you again. When your mother died, I thought you would come back and I could make peace with you and tell you my story. Marion, I am so sorry for the pain I must have caused you when you were growing up. I was so ignorant of your needs and ambitions I just wallowed in my own troubles. I was so proud when I heard you became a doctor, without any support or a family to back you up. I am ashamed of the way I let you down. I pray you will have some understanding of the reasons behind my silence.

As you know, I never knew my mother and she was no part of my life. No photos, nothing to show she had ever existed. The only time my father ever mentioned her was when he told me he loved her more than any other living thing, not that he didn't care for me, he did, but I never could fill his aching heart. That was the way it was between us. It was like my mother stood there, keeping us apart like a jilted lover.

It was the day a kid at school called me black and punched me in the face, saying, 'Why wasn't I living with my tribe?' I ask my father the question 'Did my mother have black skin?' His answer was 'Yes' then he walked away with his head low. I didn't think that would matter to my life, but it did. I got more and more insults, specially from the Hartnells and Smiths, always getting roughed up after school, coming home with grazed knees and bruises everywhere.

My father would stitch up my ripped clothes saying, 'If they had known Betty, they would know how beautiful she was, the dumb bastards.' I was much older before I learned the tragedy that took my mother's life. I feel I must tell you about Betty's death. There was an old wash house out the back near the back door. My father pulled it down and extended the brick building out to the side as it is now. A new laundry and your bedroom. The wash house was where she did it. My father explained the image he was confronted with just before his death. He found his beloved wife hanging from a rafter, the rope tight around her neck. Remembering the image every day ate away his heart and soul. I was three when it happened. They had lost my sister a short time before.

I am sorry I have to tell you this, but it is your heritage. I have never been ashamed of being part aboriginal, in fact, I was proud. It was always kept quiet because of the prejudice against people with dark skin. My father had put up with the indignities from the first day he fell in love with Betty and she became his wife. There were days I wish I could have known her. My father never talked about her. The only information I have is what I have passed on to you. He never wanted me to have to experience the intolerance of the Born and Bred that was shown to him. As I would never have wanted you to be faced with such bigotry. Though most that did know anything about that part of the MacKenzie history are gone now, there are only the lurking secrets hidden in the fibre of Ravens Hollow.

As far as I know, the Born and Bred never found out about my biggest betrayal I bestowed on you and your poor mother. Dottie was a good person, as you know and before taking to her bed, we were happy in our own way and we loved you and wanted the best for you. Dottie and I had history. Being Born and Bred, our families were good friends and marriage was a natural progression. I had the store to take over from my father and Dottie's parents were over the road in their store. You arrived and that was the way it was meant to be. I became more and more interested in my mother's people and started to go out to her mob. That's where I met Isobel.

My weakness was my crime. Marion, you have a brother. His name is George. He is twelve years younger than you. It destroyed your mother. She was so ashamed. That is why she took to her bed and only got out when she knew I was in the store, or you were at school. My guilt weighs heavy on me for hurting you and your mother.

George and his mother, Isobel, gave me feelings I had never experienced before. The happiness and the elation I felt watching him being born, it was pure joy. Isobel didn't want her mob to see our son being born in case he was too white. Normally birthing was women's business. She was a strong one with a mind of her own.

Only wanting me. She needn't have worried about the colour of his skin. He was black. Her mob accepted us both. I spent as much time as I could with them, my second family.

I was surprised you never seemed to miss me when I wasn't around. When George was older, I bought them a house in Newtown. The address is on the back of the envelope. It is my greatest wish that when you read this letter, you would find George. He always said he would wait there until he could meet his sister. It is my fond hope you can meet your brother and become friends. I stayed with your mother until she died. I had hoped you would have come back some time. I didn't realise we had hurt you so much when we made you leave. There was no other solution. It had to be that way. You couldn't have stayed.

When you wouldn't come home for her funeral, I knew I had lost you forever. My heart was broken. I know it was my punishment. I wanted too much from life and didn't give enough back. I should have made more of an effort to look after you. You were a child when you left and I had no idea what you had to face. I did expect you to come back after it was over. You never told me you had a university placement to study medicine.

My plan for you was to come back and marry David and everything would be as it was meant to be. I am so sorry for my complete ignorance of your needs and your plans for your future. They were different to mine. I read an article about you in the Herald, about an award you received for your work with aboriginal children in Alice Springs early in your career. Pride welled up in me. It was then I realised I had no right to that pride.

I thought it was ironic you were drawn to work with the people that were part of your heritage and you wouldn't have known why. I played a part in destroying both your lives—my wife and my daughter. My only legacy is George. I always did right by him. The Ravens Hollow property is yours to do with as you will. George is well provided for too.

If only I could have told you my story when you were twenty-one as I had planned, things may have been different. Happiness may have been ours. In my naïvety I wish we could have come together before my death. As I write this, I have lost hope as my time is almost over. I will go to my grave without your forgiveness.

Your Loving Father

James Robert MacKenzie

Perspiration ran down Marion's face sitting in this dark, damp room her great-grandfather had dug into the rock. She had never asked any questions about her family. She had just lived in the present. David and her girlfriends filled her mind. Even when Dottie took to her bed, she never really read too much into it. She was a child with a child's mind. Why didn't she ask? She read the letter again and then again. Her comprehension was slow to take it all in. She had a brother; she had indigenous blood. Why didn't she know? How could she have been so blind? Maybe she could die right now and not have to face her father's story.

Her emotions were riding a roller coaster. She was swinging between love and hatred for her father. How could he pile all his problems onto her? How could he have kept this from her? Why didn't he tell her before she left? Why did she need to know all this? Someone else owned this story. It didn't belong to her.

It was an hour before she dragged herself up the stairs, clutching the letter in her hand. Why didn't he tell her before? They could have faced the boy, his mother, and her mother together. Why didn't he post the letter years ago? He would have been able to find her. Why didn't she come back? Why did she let her hurt and disappointment destroy the chance to have her parents in her life? No, they had let her down when she had needed them. Why would she feel guilty?

Marion had counselled patients in her practice about how to handle family situations for years. She thought she had heard it all. What gave her the right when she couldn't face her own truths? Was her father a weak, selfish man? She always blamed her mother for the uneasy situation in their home. Why didn't she ask why? Didn't she help? Because she was a child. It was their responsibility, not hers.

She laid on her bed and cried. Why was the end of her life being so cruel to her? She had been a good person, being helpful and caring. Why was she being punished this way?

Marion's mind was exploding. Her hand went to her hair, her once thick black curly hair she had tried to straighten. Why didn't someone say, why? And her dark eyes, so alien to her Scottish background, why didn't someone say? She couldn't believe she never asked. Feeling it now, grey thinning hair, she cried for those black curls she hated so much. How she wished she could have it back. She cried for her mother.

For some reason, James Robert thought no one knew about Isobel and the boy. Dottie would know the spy network would never miss such immoral indiscretion by a Born and Bred. It had been the shame that sent Dotti to her bed, never wanting anyone to see her face again.

For the first time in her life, Marion felt she was completely alone. Even when she had to leave her home, she had a strength that kept her able to face the challenges. She had always been so strong and independent. Now she prayed she would be able to keep going until she got out of this place that had only caused her pain. The layers of her emotions reached a depth of despair.

The voice called to her noor-boorp (child) warr (raven). 'Was it because of the child?' Marion thought, as she fell into a deep sleep and dreamed of the life she would have had if the cross she had to bear had never been placed in her story.

15

MARION'S ANGUISH:
A LIFE LOST—A LIFE FOUND

Wolnoit-yere-bil (family). The voice echoed in Marion's drowsy head. Slowly, she remembered the letter. If only she had known, would it have change anything? As Dr Marion MacKenzie, she was passionate about her work and every day was filled with enthusiasm and dedication. She believed in her purpose. She never looked for anything else.

The plans she had with David could never have come true after the incident in the drain. That couldn't just go away as her father had indicated in his letter. Just come back and marry David and it would all be forgotten. She had to decide if she would find George, George MacKenzie. She repeated the name over and over, her brother or her half-brother.

She would take her medication, an hour drive both ways. Could she make it? She was saving that drive to get back to Melbourne. She doubted whether it would be worth the effort. He wouldn't know her; she wouldn't know him. It would be a disappointment and bring her more sorrow. George might not be at that address anymore. It would be a gamble, a waste of time. With a clearer head, she felt she had no choice. She would head off to Newtown to find George MacKenzie.

Marion remembered the drives to Newtown with Bert and Claudia. Once in a while they would take her, Jenny and Jessica, to do window shopping; maybe buy a new dress or shoes for a special occasion and a milk shake or ice cream in the milk bar. It was one of the good times in those days, with the sisters. The drive was bringing back those memories. Sometimes she would go with her father if he had to see a wholesaler. She always enjoyed those trips. Her nerves were telling her this visit might not be as pleasant.

Marion saw the familiar landscape. There seemed to be little change apart from a winery popping up almost around every corner and the upgraded road. But the landscape and the farmland were still there. Her heart softened as she saw the dry conditions. She felt as if she were driving into the past again. She found the address easily, as she had some idea where it was. It was like she had never been away.

An early fifties cream brick stood there like the day it was built. He was in the front yard with a small boy, showing the boy the flowers, bending down to his level and seeming to be explaining something to him. He took the boy's hand and lead him to the next plant. Marion felt like a stranger to herself. She slowly got out of the car.

George looked up and hurried over to the gate, 'I knew you would come. I told Toby: Marion might come today.' His black face beamed, with tears in his eyes.

'Hello George, I am your sister.' Marion was shocked at her words. George opened the gate and the natural hug seemed so comfortable. They both smiled. He took Marion inside after he had introduced her to Toby, his five-year-old grandson.

'I look after Toby while his mum is at work. He will be off to school soon and I won't have much to do.' He patted Toby on the head. 'Do ye want to go and play while I talk to ye Aunty Marion?'

'He is a lovely boy. I have never been called aunty before, or sister for that matter. This is all so new to me.' Marion trembled.

'I'll make you a cup of tea. You look a little pale.' Marion sat at the retro table, green laminex everywhere.

'You live my yourself then?'

'No, me daughter lives here too. We both lost our partners. Me wife died years ago and me girl's husband got killed on his motor bike just before Toby was born. We get on well. We are good for each other.' George brought the tea over to the table and sat down. 'Our father told me he had hurt you, but always hoped you would come back. He knew where you lived, but he said it had to be your choice. If you didn't want to see him, he didn't want to force himself on you.'

Marion couldn't reply. A lifetime of arrogance and stupidity kept this family apart. 'How did you know it was me when I pulled up, George? I am sure I don't look the same as I did. It's been so long. If you saw a photo, it would have been when I was a young girl.'

George giggled like a child. 'Why wouldn't I know me own sister? Our spirits don't change.' He smiled, taking her hand. 'You are not well, I can see. Do you need to lie down? I am here now to look after you.'

Marion blurted out everything about her illness. She couldn't understand why she wanted to tell him. She had always kept herself a closed book to outsiders, but George wasn't an outsider, was he? Marion felt comfortable telling her brother she had only a few months to live. Until now, she had accepted it with grace, but she had the strongest feeling she wanted to live.

'Will you be able to stay to meet me girl? She knows I have been waiting for ye all these years.'

'Yes; I would love to meet my niece.' Marion's stomach churned. A niece, a brother, and a great-nephew. It was so much to take in. She almost cried. A gap in her life she never knew was there, was closing… and the child. What had she missed?

Now it was too late. It was a slow drive back to the Hollow, with warm feelings surrounding her. She was surprised the meeting was so easy. It was as if they had met before. Marion knew blood ties were strong. She had learned from many of her patients the strength that can be gained from family members, but didn't expect it from a brother and sister that had never known each other.

They had arranged to meet again and exchanged phone numbers. George said he would come to her next time, to save her the drive.

Marion wondered if David or his father had known about George. And her father had two families he was looking after! Why didn't someone tell her?

As she entered the back door, she decided to go into her old room. The door was locked. She had never locked it. Why would it be locked now? Where would the key be? She felt along the architrave above the door. It was jammed in a crack. She unlocked it and slowly opened the door to her old sanctuary. Marion had trouble focusing for a minute. Finding the light switch, she walked back into her childhood.

The room was as she had left it. She felt as though she had just come in from school. She sat at her dressing table and saw her brush with the remains of black curly hair. How carefree she had been with all her dreams. There had been times in the past fifty years she had wondered what David was doing or where he was. He'd had papers printed in The Australian Medical Journal from time to time, so she knew he was successful and seemed to be travelling around a lot. She liked to have some idea where he was, so she could make sure she never ran into him. Why did she think it would matter to him anyway, after she left without even saying goodbye?

He had never tried to contact her. She was sure he would have been able to find her. He could have asked her father. It was getting easier now with the new technology. Anyway, the yellow pages always had her name printed as bold as brass. Her clothes were hanging in the wardrobe, the drawers still full. She sat and went through everything, remembering things she had long forgotten. Her father must have expected her back. As his letter said, she had let him know she had the university placement; that she had deferred for a year. He just didn't understand the outside world.

Sadness surrounded Marion. Her young mind could not forgive that easily. The bed was made up with clean sheets. James Robert really had expected her back. She opened the window to let the fifty-year-old air out and the fresh air in. She would be leaving her mother's storeroom and be sleeping down here until she left.

It had been a confusing day, feeling emotions that had been dead to her. A new world was opening up for Marion, but it was all too late. As she laid her head down on her childhood bed, she felt a comfort. Her age and disease had disappeared. The voice was louder and closer, Moo-roop (spirit) moomg-roon (alive). Marion knew it was Betty now, a friend that had been with her, a guide, an angel that had always been there, but she never knew why. If only her angel had the power to save her for a little longer, so she could have some time with her newly acquired family.

16

REGRETS AND CONSEQUENCES: UNSPOKEN PERCEPTIONS

Marion woke feeling drained from the day she'd had with George. She hoped Chas Palmer didn't ring today to say his work was finished. Not wanting to leave now, needing to see George again. There was a renewed confidence. She wasn't sure why.

They were there today, sitting, staring. What did they want from her? They must know she hated the hard-hearted bullies that they became. Maybe they wanted to apologise for their brutality. She chuckled to herself.

She planned to visit Jessica today, but she would have to wait for them to leave. Not wanted to face them under any circumstances. She would tidy up the storeroom while she waited for them to leave. Did some hand washing in the laundry. Been able to get some coat hangers out of her room and hang the clothes on what was left of the old Hills Hoist her father had installed so long ago. Marion was starting to feel like she was home when she was at the clothesline.

The Ravens circled gently around her, one brushing its wing softly on her cheek. She chuckled for the second time today. Her surroundings were starting to feel so familiar. Was it Betty or George that was making her have a different attitude today? She waved to the ravens as she went inside.

Marion moved the few things she had brought with her from her mother's room down to her childhood sanctuary. She only had to have a look in the corner cupboard in the storeroom that was covered by a heavy, dusty curtain. It was obvious it had not been moved for some time.

Marion didn't remember seeing it there when she was younger. Maybe it had a cupboard in front of it, hiding away her mother's secret treasures. She chuckled again. If she didn't know better, she would think she had had too much to drink today. Holding her nose, she pulled back the curtain. There were three old boxes stacked on top of each other. 'I may not get to visit Jessica's today,' she thought to herself.

Taking the top box over to the bed, she removed the lid cautiously, as if she expected it to explode. She stared at the diary wrapped in an old lace hanky. She felt her mother standing behind her, waiting for her courage to kick in before she could stop her hands trembling to open it. Dottie's notebook had little bits and pieces jotted down. Jumping from page to page, there was nothing that made sense to Marion until she came to the last page. The hand- writing was wobbly and hard to read.

Dear Marion,

I am very sick and I have no will to live any longer. I pray I can join my mother and father and be safe in their arms. Your father is a bad man. He hurt me so much and made me ashamed to be called a MacKenzie. I just wanted to hide my shame from the eyes of Ravens Hollow and pay your father back. The best way I could do that was to be cruel to you. That hurt him more than me hiding away. Consequently, all I did to myself was to create more shame and guilt. My hate ate away at me so much that I lost everything.

If only I had the courage to have faced the problem of your father's infidelity. I am a weak woman. If only I was given the courage that Betty had and hung myself from the rafter. It would have been better for everyone. Saying sorry won't undo all the misery I have brought you. It was your father I hated, not you, dear Marion. I have a dark heart. I deserve to rot in hell.

Dotti Barns MacKenzie

Marion threw the book down and cried. Why couldn't she have helped her mother? Why didn't someone tell her? Why didn't her father get help for her? Marion knew she would never have the answers to her questions and it was all too late. She wondered why she was getting loaded up with rubbish that did not belong to her. She had just been a bystander in this soap opera. That's what she always had preferred to believe.

She had been as weak as her parents, not confronting her own problems. She was just as keen to escape the Hollow's prying eyes and hide her shame. They encouraged her to go, but she didn't fight. She didn't tell David she was as weak as Dottie and James Robert.

Marion brought the next box over to the bed. This one was bigger, so she was expecting more than a book. Her eyes misted over again as she saw a photo of herself when she was first born on the top of others of her growing up with dates relating to the times and her age. There were photos of her birthdays that had been celebrated in the family's happy times.

She remembered the birthday when she got her first watch and feeling sophisticated and grown up. And there was her bike that let her go out of town, down bush tracks, exploring the countryside and riding through the forest. How she loved the forest! The freedom riding her bike gave her was exhilarating. That was before Dottie took to her bed. After that, it was a form of escape and didn't have the same thrill.

Under the photos were baby clothes, each year of age tied with ribbon. Maybe Dottie had hoped for another baby. When she heard about her husband fathering a child with another woman, that would have been hard to tolerate. There were so many things Marion would never be able to understand. She was seeing a different side to her mother; the one she never had a chance to know. If she had come back, she may have known her as woman to woman, instead of child and parent.

If only she had come home and put her hurt and disappointment aside for the welfare of her family—maybe she was the one with the dark heart. Marion wondered how she had been so kind and caring to strangers all these years, when she had turned her back on her mother and father. The last fifty years were spent walking in the shoes of a woman she had created, believing she was the victim. And yes, she was. She was robbed of so much. She now realised she had taken out her revenge on the wrong ones.

Marion put the next box on the bed. It was lighter than the others. She thought it might be empty. Feeling strained, she wasn't sure if she could cope with what would confront her now. Marion was pleasantly surprised. It was a music box. Turning it over, she saw the engraved words, 'Jane Cameron, Edinburgh Scotland'. Marion was struck by the beauty of this antique piece and presumed it had belonged to Robert MacKenzie's wife. She must have brought it from Scotland with her.

She had heard some stories as a child about her great-grandmother. Marion wound up the music box and walked out to see if they had gone. Relieved, she opened the door to the veranda and sat in the rocking chair. She lifted the lid to hear the Celtic music drift through the air.

She didn't see the petite woman with the bonnet tied with the blue ribbon standing in the corner, smiling. Marion sat there for some time. The music had stirred her and sent her mind in another direction. Her heritage was so diverse; the meeting of cultures she had never acknowledged. Sadness overcame her as she realised the hardships the MacKenzie women had endured, all at the hands of the MacKenzie men and this arbitrary, cynical, treacherous town of Ravens Hollow.

17

MARION'S CHANGING WORLD: THE SHADOWS OF DEATH BRING AWAKENINGS

Wolnoit-yere-bil (family) Betty was saying as Marion woke. If only she had known what the messages were all these years. She hoped they weren't there, sitting staring up at the veranda. She wondered why they were there some days and not others. Marion pulled herself up. Why did she think of them at all?

She wanted to tell Jessica about George today. Her strength was still there, and she enjoyed the short stroll to the cottage. As Marion opened the gate to Mabel Burns Cottage, she wondered how many people knew the stories connected to the cottage. Had they faded or had they grown into more untruths as most stories did?

She was sure there had been no documented, accurate history recorded. The only thing that could be proof of the things that happened so many years ago was the baby's cry. Marion found Jessica in the back garden today and was taken away by the beauty Jessica had managed to create amid a long drought. The old friends hugged longer than normal, clinging to each other, clinging to their past.

'Your garden is beautiful,' Marion said, delighted with the array of colour.

'It is all I have now. Mum left behind quite a mess, as you can imagine. I never had time when I was working and looking after my boys to garden. Funny how life changes and you find what you have been looking for—such a simple thing, my garden. Now it has become my passion.' Jessica's face gleamed.

Marion was happy for her school friend. They sat at a table and chairs under the shade of an enormous tree. They would never know its roots went down into the depths of the earth that had been Nurse Mabel Burns's burial well for so many little souls.

The pair chatted, and Jessica filled Marion in about all the gossip and goings on in the town—the same old stories about the bad Smiths and Hartnells still up to their old tricks. Marion secretly hoped other young girls weren't hurt the way she had been.

The Hollow was a place that seemed to stay the same, ignoring the progress of the world. Marion wanted to approach the subject of George. She was curious to hear if there had been rumours at the time of her mother taking to her bed. She nervously asked, 'Jessica, did you ever hear about my father having another woman in his life?'

Jessica smiled. 'We were children, Marion. I never really knew if any of the stories were true until I came back and people asked me if I had seen you, and did you run away because you found out about your father's other woman.' Marion couldn't speak. All these years she had lived in ignorance of the affair.

'Why didn't someone tell me? I blamed my mother all these years. If only I had known.' Marion sank back in her chair. 'All the time I was away enjoying my life, thinking I was so good, the bright one. I was a saint caring for the sick when I could have come back and helped my mother; relieved her pain and suffering. No, I was off helping strangers.' Shame and bile rose in Marion's throat.

'That means David would have known when we were going out together and he never said anything. Have you ever talked to him since you came back?' Marion asked Jessica.

'Yes, I see him all the time. We chat occasionally. He thought your father's behaviour may have been the reason you left in such a hurry, or that you hated him because he was going to Sydney without you.'

'No, it was neither of those reason.' Marion became withdrawn.

'Have you tried to see David?' Jessica felt she had let her friend down.

'No, I haven't had the courage. When I think of him, I feel like a teenager again and lose all my confidence.' Marion had to giggle. She still saw him as he was the last time she looked into his eyes. She wondered if he had deteriorated as much as she had.

'You must try. He would be so pleased to see you.' Jessica was serious now. 'I am surprised you haven't run into him. He is always out and about.' Jessica smiled remembering the fun times they all had together. David and Marion were a natural couple.

'I only go to the supermarket to get a few things to keep me going until I head back to Melbourne. I just nick in and out. I don't know anyone here now, so I keep my eyes down.' Marion buried her face in her hands for a minute. Little did she know there had been eyes on her from day one of her return. Even the ones who didn't know her knew the stories.

'I have something to tell you. I went to Newtown and met my brother,' Marion said proudly.

'Is that true? A child was never mentioned in the gossip I heard. How did you find out about this Ravens Hollow scandal?' Jessica asked with interest.

'My father left me a letter that waited fifty years for me to open.' Tears filled her eyes.

'Marion, none of your family's misdemeanours were your responsibility. It is not your weight to carry. You were only an innocent bystander.' Jessica tried to comfort her friend.

'The story hasn't ended yet, Jessica. My brother has a black mother. The woman my father loved was an aboriginal and I found out my grandmother was aboriginal too.' The softness in Marion's voice was one of love.

Jessica didn't speak. There was a long silence between the two old school friends. Jessica didn't want Marion to see any bias in her face, but she was surprised Marion seemed to accept the black heritage without question.

'I will never understand why my father never told me before I left. I would have come back. I let my disappointment in my parents deprived me of a family.' Tears filled Marion's eyes again.

'My brother is a beautiful man. He has a daughter and a grandson. I want to spend as much time as I can with them before I leave.' Marion couldn't hide her pain. If only she had more time, if only if she had known.

They sat under the tree; the leaves swaying with the slight breeze. 'Jessica, I have rambled on about all my problems. I never asked you how you coped with your loneliness.' Marion suddenly felt selfish.

'Oh, I don't feel lonely. They are with me, my boys. Ravens Hollow has a way of letting spirits roam free, the ones that are taken before their time.' Jessica smiled. Marion knew she had Betty, her angel voice. It appeared she wasn't the only one that had someone with her.

A peace came over Marion. Sharing George with Jessica made him real, a real living brother. 'George will be coming to visit me before I go back to Melbourne. I hope you have a chance to meet.' Marion's voice took on a different tone when she mentioned George.

'I would be pleased to meet him. You are welcome to bring him here to my haunted cottage.' They both laughed.

Jessica walked to the front gate with Marion. There was a faint cry in the background. 'I have never heard that before. I was never sure if it was true.' Marion smiled. 'Maybe you never really listened.' Jessica's voice sounded as though it came from a deep tunnel.

'Do you think Bert and Claudia are out there in a parallel dimension, their spirits floating? Claudia wouldn't like the damp musty smell in those old mining tunnels or shafts.' Marion's scientific mind and common logic would never have thought or said those words.

Just as she stepped out the gate, Jessica said, 'When are you going to tell me why you left without a word?' Marion felt a chill pass over her. She couldn't answer for a moment.

'Soon, maybe,' were the only words that would come out of her mouth.

Marion was tired but uplifted after their chat. Jessica had always been there for her in their younger days. She never imagined she would be relying on her again. As she neared the store, she saw them sitting there. Thomas was with them today. They were looking up at the French doors, staring, waiting. For what, Marion wondered? She never wanted to look at their faces again. Maybe it was them that kept her away. Blaming her parents was an easy way out of confronting her real problem.

Marion cut through Mill Street into the back of the property. They would have seen her. She knew they would have a smirk on their faces. Why are they there? What more could they take from her? They had robbed her of her soul.

Anger rose in her. She felt like a volcano ready to explode and spread hot lava all over this stinking town. Hurrying into her sanctuary. She was a child again. Laying on her narrow bed that she had always kept near the window. She looked up at the old holland blind. Fifty years of dust was thick along the top. If she pulled it down, it would go all over the bed. She would leave it until the morning. Another day wouldn't matter. It had been like it since she opened the door. She had been so glad to have her old room back. It didn't seem to matter.

In her other life, Marion's cleaner, the lovely Mrs Monson, came every day and made her surgery and home sparkle. Now she was living in this filthy old room, with sheets and covers that had been waiting to be laid on for fifty years. Like Jessica's tree, Marion's tree outside her bedroom window was surviving the drought and stood as tall and strong as she remembered as a child.

She watched the orange glow of the setting sunshine through the negative spaces between the leaves. She had watched that tree from the first day of her life that she could remember; how it changed with the seasons, the beauty of its bare branches in the winter. She loved the mystical forms and shadows it created, the changing colours of the autumn and the blossom in spring. She was always disappointed when she had to watch the pretty pink flowers fall.

Now, it was a deep green in defiance of the drought. She watched the glow of the negative space change into darkness as she was falling asleep. She remembered Jessica's face when she told her of her black brother and grandmother. Marion knew she tried to hide her shock, but it was obvious. Marion silently thanked her friend. Funny, Marion thought, it seemed to answer something she had always wondered about: why she had dark eyes and hair, so alien to her Scottish heritage. She smiled as she fell into sleep. Betty had been telling her these secrets all her life.

18

ELEVATING THE SPIRIT: FACING TRUTHS, FINDING PEACE

Marion woke. She enjoyed Betty's voice. It soothed her somehow, giving her strength to face the day. Looking at her tree in the morning light, she could see the green leaves were black with the ravens sitting on every branch.

George had been to visit twice now. The first time, opening the store door with his own key, calling out before coming up the stairs. Marion was surprised he had a key to the property. Their father had been gone for so long. George explained how James Robert had got him a job as a storeman at one of the wholesalers he dealt with in Newtown. When he left school and on the weekends, he would come and help their father to prepare the store for the following week. He also told her how they had cleaned and locked her bedroom door for the time she would return.

George would have known her father much better than she ever had. She felt the sting of sibling rivalry, another emotion Marion had never experienced. There had been so many feelings she never knew existed. She felt she must have been made of stone. That's how she had survived. Marion realised she had built so many protective walls around herself, she had forgotten who she really was. Maybe she never really knew; they had taken that away from her.

The solicitor had completed all the tasks that were needed and she had signed all the papers giving the child the legal right to inherit the MacKenzie property, to do with whatever she wanted. There was nothing more she had to do except to explain to George and Jessica why she had left her home and why her dreams had been stolen from her. This would be her last day in Ravens Hollow. She would escape tomorrow back to Melbourne and prepare for her death.

Marion was going to set out a light lunch. George was going to bring camp chairs and a table. It was going to be a lovely day to spend under her tree with her brother and friend. If only she had more time. If only she had known. Everything was ready when Jessica came in the side gate.

Luckily, there was no evidence the ravens been in the tree earlier. Marion didn't have a plan for how to tell her story. She wasn't even sure she would be able to relive it, even though she remembered everyday detail.

Jessica and George were getting on well. Marion hoped they would stay friends when she was gone. Marion had an expensive white wine to go with lunch, thinking it might give her some Dutch courage to tell her story. Their chit-chat was light and friendly, just like old friends having lunch in the sunshine. Marion thought, 'The world is too lovely to leave.'

'I will be leaving tomorrow.' Marion's voice was shaking. They both stared, their smiles suddenly gone.

'So soon?' George's face almost turned grey.

'I will miss you so much,' Jessica's eyes watered.

'It is time. All my arrangements have been made. I need to get back to Melbourne. I will be sorry to leave you two. You have made this time the best.' Marion's eyes watered too.

'I feel I owe you an explanation why I left the Hollow as I did and could never come back. Though from what I have learned lately, I should have been back here for many reasons. You are one George. But I could never have imagined you existed. I was just too weak.' Marion trembled.

George and Jessica could see Marion was struggling.

'Do you need to lie down for a while?' George asked.

'No, No. I have to go on. You must know the truth.' The wine was kicking in, giving Marion the strength she needed. Just get on with it and get the job done.

'I was so in love with David, I would have followed him to the ends of the earth. I know you knew that, Jessica, and I knew you would be surprised when I deserted him. It broke my heart.' Marion started to ramble a bit about David and their plans—how they wanted to work together all over the world and into the outback to make a difference. She did do that. Wondering if David ever did. She knew he had achieved many things without her. Seeing articles. She had been successful too. Why did they have to do it alone?

'It was the afternoon David told me he was going to Sydney without me. I was disappointed, but I was happy to go to Melbourne by myself and wait for him. I hadn't told my parents anything about my university placement in the medical school. I had twelve weeks before I had to be there. Having to find the right moment, and I was having trouble finding that moment. My mother wouldn't have cared, but I thought my father may have been upset. He always said he wanted me to help in the store. Knowing I was going to disappoint him.'

George went to interject but decided to sit up and listen

'I stayed with David too long and it was clouding over and the dusk became dark. I thought I would cut through the drain to save time. The minute I stepped into the tunnel, I knew I had done the wrong thing. That was the minute my life would never be the same. They followed me in. It was as if they had been waiting for the day I walked in there. I was so scared, I froze. Leon Smith and Rex Hartnell walked up, one on each side of me, taking my arms. My legs went weak. They were dragging me deeper into the drain. Why did I take the shortcut? Why?

I started to scream, but they soon put a stop to that. Rex took a hanky out of his pocket and tied it around my mouth. I was so scared. I could hardly breathe.'

"So, Miss Fancy Pants, we finally have you to do what we want. We are going to take you down a peg or two, so you find out you are no better than us, the bad ones. That's what you call us, don't you? Who are you to bad mouth us, you black bitch, looking down at us with your up-turned nose? You bitch, you and your fancy boyfriend! So perfect. So clean. So good! Well, we are here to dirty you up a bit, teach you a few lessons we're sure your David couldn't teach you. You will no longer be untouchable. We plan to touch you everywhere, places David never would, and I bet you will love it and beg for more."

Jessica's eyes widened not sure she wanted to hear she saw George's face almost go white.

'They took it in turns to shout those words at me. They were hanging on to my arms so hard I couldn't move. They laid me gently on the ground. I thought they were going to leave me then, but to my surprise, they started to rip off my clothes. I laid there naked. Surely, they will leave me now, I thought. They have had their fun. I would never have been able to imagine what they were about to do to me next. I was really so naïve I never knew another person could be so cruel to their own kind. My innocence was taken away in seconds. Rex held me down with his knees on my shoulders. "Go for it, Leon! You can go first. I bet she is a virgin, you lucky bugger."

I still didn't know what was going to happen until I felt him on top of me. The violation was excruciating. The pain outweighed the humiliation. It seemed to go on forever, Rex yelling, "Hurry up. I want a turn!" Before long, Rex was there thumping me like I wasn't human. The abuse was horrific. I couldn't believe what was happening to me. The violation, aggression, and physical harm they caused me was nothing to what they did to my mind. I have never really been the same after that evening in the drain. They left me after they went at me more than once. I was so shocked it took me a while to realise what had happened.

When I finally could stand up, I struggled home with semen and blood running down my legs. I was terrified. How did this horror happen to me? I knew I would have to creep in the back door to the bathroom as quietly as I could. Dad hadn't closed the store, so I had time to bathe. There were no marks on me. They had been careful not to leave any signs. I would have to keep this secret. I decided never to acknowledge it had ever happened. I was hesitant to see David; I was so ashamed, so I pretended to have a cold for a few days.'

Jessica was finding it hard not to cry. The images that were before her eyes were something she would never forget.

'When I eventually saw him, I am sure he must have thought there was something wrong. I suppose he thought I was upset about him going to Sydney. I went through the days in a daze. It was like I was walking in a thick fog. It wasn't long before I realised I was going to have a baby. I had so many symptoms that David and I had read about in his father's medical books. I had to tell someone. That was the hardest thing I ever had to do.

I went to my mother, saying I was sure I was pregnant. She never asked how it happened or who was the father. She just yelled at me, "Get out of my sight! You are just like your father! Get out, get out and never come back!" Her voice was evil. I walked out and never saw her again.

I was devastated, so I had to tell my father. He was a little more sympathetic and said he would make arrangements. The next morning, he came to my room and gave me the address of the Methodist Babies Home in South Yarra. I had to get ready to leave on the early bus.

I had no time to think. I threw a few things in a bag and was at the bus stop in time. My father never asked me anything about who the father was or when I would be having the baby. Not one thing. He just said, "I am sorry, Marion. This is all I can do for you," handing me some money. My disappointment left me hollow inside. I cried all the way to Melbourne.

I found the home and that was that. My shame was hidden away from the world. I was wanted by nobody. There I sat and stared out the window, scared to death as to what was going to happen to me. I knew nothing about what the birth of a baby entailed, only what David and I had read in his father's medical books. It seemed I knew more than other young girls I shared a dormitory with. They all had horror stories to tell. My eyes became open to a world I could never imagined existed.

We did get some insight as to what was going to happen to us, but the main thing was we were brainwashed to believe the baby had to be adopted out to a proper family that could give it the benefits of a family life. The babies would never have to know they had been illegitimate. I am ashamed to say I didn't want the child. I didn't need to be convinced. It was like a growth I wanted to get rid of and forget any of it had ever happened.

I was in for a shock. The birth wasn't easy, which made me hate the baby more. I never looked at it. They said it was a girl and she was whisked away. That was it, or so I thought. I didn't count on the emotions that would follow and the emptiness and pining I had for her. I didn't hate her at all. I only hated how she got into me. She became a separate identity to the growth I felt in my body. I became so confused and slipped into a deep depression. They told me she had gone to a good home and I should be proud I could give a childless couple this great gift.'

Jessica was beside herself with Marion's grief. She knew what it was like to lose a child. She wanted to get out of her chair and put her arms around her old school friend.

'It was some time before my body and mind were well enough for me to be able to leave the home. As luck would have it, my place at the university was waiting for me and I thought the horror year of my life would be behind me.

My one hope was I would never run into David. I heard he was still in Sydney. So, life took on a new journey and I slowly put the last year in a bubble and hid it away. I never could forget the child. She was never to know my name and there was never a father mentioned, so I never expected to hear about the episode again.

Every day I have wondered about the child and her wellbeing. It has been a cloud hanging over me all these years. The one good thing that came out of my experience is that I never let the cruelty I endured happen to any girl that came through my surgery door. I helped to get the adoption laws and choices for the mothers changed. The child will inherit this property. I hope you don't mind, George, but the arrangements were under way before I knew you existed and I know our father had looked after you well.' Marion was having trouble getting those last words out. She was getting tired. 'I have never been able to tell anyone my story. Thank you for listening, my brother and my school friend. I am so lucky to have had you by my side.'

Marion smiled a smile George would never forget.

George went to say something, but Marion seemed to be having trouble breathing. He scooped her up in his arms. 'Get the doctor Jessica, quickly!' George screamed, running Marion inside to her bed. He laid her down, his arms still around her. She was limp. He could feel the life going out of her.

'You have made my last weeks the best in my life, George. I love you, my brother,' Marion whispered into George's ear.

'Hang on, the doctor will be here,' George whispered back. 'You will be in my heart forever,' George cried.

They clung together, their cheeks touching, drinking in each other's tears that flowed together like a stream. They stared into each other's eyes like they were looking into the shattered souls that were the remnants of the MacKenzie clan.

'If I only had more time, if only I had known, I could have got the job done,' were Marion's last words. Before she closed her eyes, she looked that their hands clasped together, one white one black, joined together as one. If only she had more time.

Jessica and David arrived just as George pulled his arms away from his sister and they just stared at a body that was once an amazing woman that had been dealt a bad hand. The three clung to each other and cried like they would never stop. They cried for the lost years they had missed.

The black birds fluttered outside the window, softly calling raven (warr war war). Darkness (borine) George heard Betty's voice. Maybe Betty could rest now too.

19

PAYING THE PRICE OF PRIDE:
THE PRICE OF UNSPOKEN WORDS

Jessica tried to fill David in between her tears, to the reason Marion had left. The three of them were devastated. It was unbelievable that James Robert had never told anyone he had sent her away. He had never told George, just pretended he never knew why she left. He always said it must have had something to do with David. *How could he have let it happen to his child? He had always been so kind to me,* George thought to himself.

'I came and asked James Robert where she was time and time again. He just said he didn't know; that he was sure she would be back soon.' David sat with his head bent, his voice trembling. 'Finally, I accepted I had disappointed her so much that she never wanted to see me again, so even when I knew she had finally made it to university, even though I was in Sydney, I never had the courage to seek her out. My pride was hurt. What a weak bastard I was, and have been all my life,' David cried.

Jessica saw them through the French doors, sitting there as if they had some right to stare at the veranda. Hate surged up in her, a hate she had never known. 'I wish I was a violent man. I would walk out there with a gun and kill them both, but I just couldn't do it. I am a weak bastard too David.' George's anger was boiling over. He felt his heart turn into a black stone. The three just stood there, staring back at the bad ones.

'How have they been allowed to enjoy their lives? How many others have they violated and caused misery to? Are the Born and Bred protecting them? The spy network would have to know how bad they were. How did they get away with it, bloody Born and Bred? But Marion and you, David, were born here. You just didn't have the same network of family members,' Jessica cried.

'We weren't a Smith or a Hartnell. They formed the foundations of Ravens Hollow,' David said, so disappointed he had devoted his life to this town. He now realised the darkness that had hovered over it; how many lives had it destroyed?

The three stood looking out the French doors and watched the Sentinels that lined every roof top on Goldsmith Way, with their heads bowed. The perpetrators had gone now, the ravens were consuming the town. The bewilderment the three felt was making it hard to face the reality of the afternoon's events. It was some time before they could move. The shock was penetrating through their bodies like a lightning bolt. Finally, David said, 'I will ring Chas Palmer to see if he has a will and I will ring Thomas to take Marion.' His professional persona was taking over, putting aside all his emotions to do his job.

George wasn't going to leave until everything was settled. He went and sat with Marion until Thomas came for her. Marion's spirit filled the room that had been her childhood sanctuary and now became her tomb. George planned to clear the room out when she was gone so no one else would be able to trespass on her world; no one else would be able to call it their sanctuary.

Jessica walked home alone. Not having a job to do except to process Marion's story. She needed to make some sort of sense of the wrong that had been visited on this kind person who had never wished anyone harm. She hoped karma would take care of Rex and Leon in some way. Why had they been able to enjoy their life the way they had? Why had her boys been taken away from her when they had been innocent of anything bad?

Another Hollow woman asking why, why, why. There would never be an answer to why the good were punished in ways that could not be comprehended. As long as the secrets of Ravens Hollow were kept away from the outside world, that was all that seemed to matter. Jessica knew she would never leave her cottage, the comfort of her crying baby and the feeling of her boys being there. But she was beginning to see the place in a different way, a haunting way. The three had arranged to meet at the local café for breakfast the next morning.

It was after dark when Thomas came for Marion. It was hard for George to let her go. 'I will look after her well,' Thomas assured George. 'I love Marion. She was so good to me.' Thomas wondered why this black man was overseeing Marion's body. He had only been a worker in the store so many years ago. George went and laid down in Dottie's storeroom. His mind churned with the disappointment he felt for his father. He would never have doubted him or the respect he had held towards him. Now he questioned what gave him the right to hide Marion away when his morality was so compromised; and what he had done to Dottie and his mother. He had looked after them in material ways. Maybe that was all his level of intellect was capable of. How could he have deserted Marion the way he did, judging her with no explanation? He must have assumed the baby was David's and he was doing the right thing for them both. Sadness engulfed him for his father and his sister. The storeroom closed in around him and he fell into a fitful sleep.

Waiting a lifetime to hold a love.

Thomas took Marion in his arms when he got her back to his parlour. 'I used to tell you I loved you, Marion. I was sure you would never return that love, but I did feel you cared in some way.' Thomas longed to kiss her, but knew it was all too late. He did that once to a teacher he had loved in his youth, but it made him sick and he didn't want that feeling to spoil his fantasy for Marion. He would make her as beautiful as he could and he thought, *I will be the last one to comfort her.* Smiling, he thought, *Maybe that's why she came back, so I could be the one to take care of her in death.*

Thomas would continue to live in the world he had created for his survival. He had always hated Rex and Leon. They were cruel to him. Even in their old age, they never missed a chance to put him down. He would never know why they had been sitting outside the parlour, staring up at the veranda of the MacKenzie building, waiting to catch a glimpse of her.

At breakfast, the three went over everything again with clearer minds, still finding it all so unbelievable that they hadn't been able to help Marion all those years ago. David's ignorant pride had deprived them of happiness and left a gaping hole in their lives. David had a copy of Marion's will and explained to the others she expected to be in Melbourne. 'But there is nothing to say we can't have her funeral here. It is just to be a private cremation and her ashes thrown to the wind. We will keep it to ourselves.' Chas would let her colleagues know of Marion's demise. He had that information. David had taken care of all the business as he would have for anyone else, just like a robot. He would break down another day.

The three brought her ashes back to the yard under her tree and as George released Marion to the wind, another extraordinary thing happened. The black birds flew under the falling ashes and carried her away in silence—a final tribute to one of Ravens Hollow's best. They wanted to right the wrong. They watched as the birds flew higher until they were dots in the sky, flying her to freedom.

Lee Ping watched with sightless eyes, smiling as he felt Marion's soul surge as she escaped the Hollow for a second time.

20

MARION'S CHILD: EXQUISITE ENIGMATIC STYLE COMES TO TOWN

As the clock ticked over into the new century, the drought broke and Central Victoria was renewed. The heavy rain washed away the dirt and grime that had accumulated over the dry months that the area had endured. Flooding water rushed down the bluestone gutters, flooding the roads with debris that had built up that nobody had bothered to clean away.

Watching from behind their lace curtains, they saw green grass appear everywhere, popping up before their eyes. Ravens Hollow was clean and green, and the sun shone on the new world.

Edwina rarely left the city, so driving out to the country was a new experience for her and Sophie. She was surprised the landscape was having an emotional effect. It was as though she was seeing the countryside for the first time. It seemed like a painting from another world with a dimension and depth she had never thought about before. So many things had happened in the last few weeks that were sending her mind in different directions.

Edwina had read about the drought but had never known the impact it had on the land or the people. So, she was happy to experience the new growth and rich colours emerging before her eyes. She couldn't wait to get to her sketch book. So many new ideas were creeping into her creative mind. 'Mum, are you sure we should be coming out here, chasing this inheritance we don't really need?' Sophie was finding the whole thing a bore and was extremely happy with the way her life was back in Melbourne.

'We have to check it out. I have no choice. It has to be dealt with one way or the other.' Edwina felt the same way as her daughter, but it seemed to be her responsibility now.

The landscape changed and a chill came over Edwina. She felt as though she was driving into a time warp. Sophie shivered. 'Are you sure we are on the right road, Edie. It's starting to scare me. Should we turn around? Let's go back home,' Sophie gasped.

'I'm following the GPS directions. We must be heading the right way.' Edwina assured her.

As they approached a darkness ahead of them, Edwina was starting to think Sophie was right. As they got closer to this black curtain they could see in front of them, they realised there were hundreds of black birds. Magically, the curtain parted and they drove through. With comfort, Edwina followed them as they guided her to their destination.

The spy network had telepathic connections, so as soon as the latest model BMW drove into Goldsmith Way, the lace curtains parted, eyes peeping through every window. Watching the two women get out of the car and stand staring at the Mackenzie building, the locals sniggered at their high heels and slim skirts, styled like they had never seen. 'They would never be able to walk in those heels around the Hollow's streets and alley ways or get their legs wide enough to jump over the gutters in those skirts,' they all thought. Why were they looking at the MacKenzie building? It must be for sale. There isn't a MacKenzie left to inherit it, or that was what the Born and Bred thought. Much of their gossip had no merit or truth, but as long as they protected the Hollow's reputation, that's all that seemed to matter.

The MacKenzie progeny wondered why they were in this strange town looking up at this formidable building in need of much care. The old bones were standing strong, though it was obvious it had weathered many a storm. Edwina had a strange feeling she had been there before. Déjà vu swept over her in waves.

Catching sight of a petite woman with a bonnet tied with a blue ribbon under her chin standing in the corner of the veranda and hearing the distant echoing bagpipe music, made Edwina's head spin. The whole experience was becoming surreal to her now. Edwina had no expectation of what she was going to be confronted with when this journey started.

Edwina Kelley-Price was a successful fashion designer. Her label *Fickle and Twisted* was known all around the world. Mother and daughter both had bad marriages over different periods in their lives and came together as partners. They were proving to be a strong team. Both their names were renowned among their peers and customers. They were rich and famous. Life was rosy. Their world was filled with hard work, decisions, plans and continuous changes, but nothing had prepared Edwina for Chas Palmer's letter.

Your birth mother, Doctor Marion Una MacKenzie, willed her Central Victorian property to you after her death last month. Edwina read and re-read the letter in detail over and over before showing it to Sophie. She had never suspected she had been adopted. The letter was a shock and it had taken days for her to make any sense of the fact she had a birth mother. Why hadn't her parents told her? It wouldn't have changed the love she had for them. They had given her a wonderful childhood and had supported her with all her dreams. She was so pleased they weren't here to be confronted with this now.

Edwina scanned the WEB for information about her birth mother's career and professional achievements, but there was nothing about her private life or the property she had inherited. The story was a mystery that left Edwina with a lot of questions she felt she would never have answers to. She thought about telling the solicitor to sell it and forget about the whole thing. But every day it intrigued her more and more.

Now standing outside the door, they needed the courage to go inside. Edwina struggled to find the key she had been sent in her deep red leather handbag, a perfect match for her dysfunctional shoes. 'Come on, Edie. I feel as if there are a million eyes piercing through me. Come on, hurry!' That Sophie was getting agitated was indicated by her high-pitched voice.

When Edwina finally produced the key, they both got the giggles. The antiquated lock and key were out of their world. They had never seen anything like it before. 'We have really gone into a time warp. I am not sure what we are going to find inside,' Edwina said, in between her laughter that was getting louder. 'Shut up. They are all watching.'

'Who? I don't see anyone.'

'I know they are there. Hurry up with that lock. Here, let me have a go.' Sophie grabbed the key.

'Would you like some help?' the women heard a deep voice ask.

Sophie swung around and looked into a face she recognised. But she couldn't have! She had never been here before. Maybe she had met him in the city.

'Do I know you?' she said in a flirtatious voice. 'No, I don't think so, but let me help you with the door. It hasn't had a lot of use lately. There is a back entrance. Have you got the key for that door? You have to go around the side street.'

'Thank you. If you could try this one, we would appreciate it.' Edwina didn't want to get too chummy.

Sophie couldn't stop herself from touching his arm as he unlocked the door.

'You have the strongest arms I have ever seen,' in her flirtatious voice again.

'Thanks,' handing her the key. 'If you need any more help you can always find me at the Golden Nugget over on Main Street.'

'Oh, we'll see you soon then.' Sophie smiled up at him.

'This might be a good place after all.' Sophie suddenly seemed very light-hearted.

Edwina couldn't believe Sophie had been so forward. She was normally shy of strangers and liked to sum them up before getting too friendly.

Stepping into the dark, damp store, the musty smell took their breath away. They had to cover their noses for a minute as they waited for their eyes to adjust to the light. They found a light switch and were amazed at the space and the height of the walls. The timber floor was still in a reasonable condition and the space was something they were always looking for. Both their minds were reeling with ideas for a country studio and warehouse.

'Wow, what a great space! Things are looking up here, Edie. We might be able to do something with this old place after all. It just needs a little fixing up and we already know a handyman.' Sophie laughed. The pair walked into the rooms that were set back into the bed rock. 'Storerooms I suppose. I can't imagine they could be used for any other purpose.' Sophie screwed up her nose.

'Look at that roll-top desk. That looks impressive. Why would it be left down here to rot? We would have to get rid of that old thing and all the other rubbish that has been left behind.' Edwina acknowledged the place had potential.

'We would need a good electrician too.'

'Your friend probably knows one,' Edwina laughed.

'Let's get upstairs and see what the house is like.' Sophie was in overdrive now.

The stairs led them into a huge living area that had no need of modernising. The French doors led out on to a veranda surrounded with decorative cast iron. They were both feeling more comfortable now. Stepping out, they could see all the way up and down Goldsmith Way and across the Main Street. The gentle perfume of the eucalyptus that lined their street helped with the musty smell of this old relic. The kitchen looked like it had come out of the Dark Ages. Sophie wondered how anyone could have lived with that workspace. There seemed to be rooms everywhere.

Like a maze, rooms had been added and changed over the years. It was hard to tell what they had been used for, or why anyone needed so many little places to hide away. The one room they both fell in love with was obviously the main bedroom with a stone fireplace. French doors led out on to a Juliet balcony, overlooking the back yard and an extremely overgrown garden.

'Can I have this room please, Edie, please?' Sophie asked with her little spoiled child voice.

'Oh, so we are moving in, are we? We will need a gardener too. Do you think your friend will know a gardener?' Edwina, laughing again.

The curtains were ripped and dusty and every wall needed painting. It would take some time to bring all this up to The Kelley-Price standard.

Sophie followed Edwina into a narrow passage at the back of the house and opened a door to a small room overlooking the same view as the main bedroom. 'You can have this room,' Sophie said to Edwina. 'And we can both see that beautiful tree change colour with the seasons.'

'Boorp-boorp boorp-boorp' (child-child), Edwina heard these words as she turned to leave the room.

'Did you hear that sound?' Edwina asked.

'What sound?' Sophie replied. 'There is another staircase. There must be a third floor.' Sophie was keen to investigate.

'You go. I need a rest. I'll wait in the car. You have the key. Lock the door and then we will find the solicitor.' Edwina's doubts about the place were returning. There seemed to be ghosts lurking.

Even though she had the strangest feeling that this was where she belonged, though the trip had unnerved her, looking around, she could feel a million eyes on her just as Sophie had. Did she need to know Marion? She would consider it another day. She wanted to get home quickly.

'What did you see on the third floor?' Edwina asked Sophie as they headed out of town.

'It was quite amazing—another storeroom or an old library, maybe. There were a lot of old legers and journals. I would just like to sit for hours and read. There is probably the history of the building and the people who lived there. You might be able to find out about your mother and father; all the secrets,' Sophie said with such enthusiasm.

'My parents were John and Mary Kelley-Price. There isn't a need to know any others!' Edwina yelled at Sophie.

'Sorry. I didn't mean to upset you.' Edwina never had spoken to her like that before.

'I want to get some ideas down that have come to me on the drive for a new range, inspired by the countryside,' Edwina's head was so full of new colours and patterns.

'Did you pick up any new ideas, Sophie?'

Sophie stared at her mother.

'Oh, maybe a bonnet with a blue ribbon,' her tone toxic.

There was no answer.

A wedge had been created.

Edwina knew she would never return.

Sophie knew she would be back.

The Sentinels flew down, circling the car, squawking as if trying to give them a message, not giving up until the mother and daughter were on the open highway.

All the eyes peeping from behind the lace curtains had wondered who the tall, dark, curly haired woman was, and was the strawberry blonde her daughter? They knew their faces but just couldn't place them. Maybe they had been to Ravens Hollow some other time.

21

SOULS THAT ARE TIED TO THEIR ROOTS OTHERS THAT DRIFT AWAY

Tears ran down Lee Ping's sightless eyes as he watched Marion's child and her daughter leave The Hollow. He cried for Marion. She, like him, had her dignity and choices taken away by an ignorant society, a society that would never learn to honour the right of a man to live according to his heart.

Sophie read for days, sitting on a cushion, looking out the window occasionally, seeing the black birds circling above the building with a message she would never understand. Maybe they didn't want her here. She felt she sort of belonged. She knew her grandmother was born here, and maybe her grandfather. Not that she had come across any evidence to indicate any truth of her mother's heritage.

She had left Edwina in the city, after she had convinced her coming back and sorting the old place out was the best option. It was easy for Sophie to persuade her the country range had to be launched at the opening of their new boutique, after the MacKenzie store was remodelled. Edwina agreed but showed no interest in coming back to Ravens Hollow.

She learned so much of the building's history and realised it was Jane

MacKenzie that stood on the veranda in the bonnet tied with the blue ribbon. She had decided to feature Jane and Hamish in the décor of the boutique. That would create local interest. Sophie had already picked up how hard it was going to be to break into the local community—that's if she needed to. Her decision for the need was a question for another day. Her target was to create a tourist market. She knew her clientele would never be the locals. This time warp was not up to wearing anything that *Fickle and Twisted* would be presenting.

The day after Sophie had read the last journal, she wandered over to the Golden Nugget to find her strongarmed man. She needed tradesmen fast. Six months later, the job was done. Even the locals peering through the store windows marvelled at the restoration this stranger had achieved. They would never see the upstairs, where Sophie's flair shone through. She had modernised most of the rooms with an elegance previous inhabitants could never have imagined.

The façade had lost nothing of its originality and charm. She could never bring herself to venture into the narrow passage leading to the room Sophie had allocated to Edwina. If she ever cared to come to Ravens Hollow, that was her mother's space. She would leave that for another day. The truth was, it scared her. The voices she was sure she imagined kept her away from that end of the house. Sophie avoided using the back entrance as much as she could.

The main bedroom became a bohemian paradise full of pink with white lace and personal treasures. It became Sophie's haven. Entering it, she was in Utopia, her world. It wasn't long after all the work had been finished, she invited Bobby Hartnell into her Utopia, falling into his strong arms and his sweet-talking words. Sophie would never learn that they shared the same grandfather.

Sophie had invited Angie, their top model, to the Hollow before the launch. She wanted to go over the procedure with her. She was missing Edwina's input, not that she was about to tell her mother that. Support from Angie would fill the gap. When Angie arrived, Sophie was surprised at the interest she had in the town.

'You seem keen to look around. I thought you would see what I have done and listen to my plans and get back to the city as soon as you could.'

'My grandmother had lived here when she was a young girl and talked about it sometimes. But would never say any more about the place when it was mentioned. The only thing she ever said was how she hated the smell of lavender. The family and I thought it was so weird we tried not to ask questions.'

'Well, I am here because my mother inherited the place. She hasn't wanted anything to do with it though, so it is my project.' Sophie didn't feel inclined to expand on any more of her business.

'I've invited one of Bobby's friends to have dinner with us tonight at the Golden Nugget, so you can see some of the culture that has been left behind in this old gold mining town.' Sophie laughed.

Angie and Oliver crept out of the spare room Sophie had decorated with her unique style just as Sophie had put Bobby's coffee on the breakfast table.

'So, you two got on OK then, it seems.' Sophie was sort of pleased but surprised.

'Yes,' Angie said, blushing a little. She wasn't usually so quick to jump into bed with someone she had just met. She just fell for his good looks and the high cheek bones and strong jaw line.

Oliver winked at Bobby with a thumbs up. And that's how it was. Sophie would be Mrs Hartnell and Angie would be Mrs Smith. That gave the Born and Bred something to talk about.

Sophie's project was an enormous success. Tourists flocked to Ravens Hollow, keeping the blow-ins in town longer than usual, with the Born and Bred pushed further into the background. They felt they were losing a grip on their position and control. The Sentinels knew something was brewing.

Angie and Sophie became pregnant at almost the same time. There would be a new Hartnell and Smith for the Hollow to contend with.

Bobby became more demanding, feeling his place in the relationship was becoming redundant. Sophie was so busy with the business and out of sorts with the baby coming, there seemed to be little room for him. He moped around like a spoiled child. Sophie lost patience with him and told him to go to the Nugget more than once.

Sophie couldn't believe he would ever hit her, but it was happening more often. It was as if he became a different person, not the man she fell in love with. She tried to talk to him about his feelings, assuring him he was so important to her and the child they would be having. Sophie concluded he was just a dumb bastard and she was stupid to be taken in by the Hartnell common charm. She made plans to leave before the birth.

Angie was having similar problems. 'I became infatuated with his looks; I know that now. We were from different worlds and he was becoming violent. He kept saying, 'Tell the preacher you love him and he will give you what you want.' He said he didn't know where that came from. I am so scared, Sophie, we must get out of here. Our babies aren't safe.' Angie pleaded with Sophie to arrange an escape. It wasn't long before the MacKenzie building was deserted again and Sophie's Utopia was dusty and cobwebs covered everything, looking like Miss Havisham's wedding table in Great Expectations.

Lee Ping watched with tears in his sightless eyes. For a short time, Ravens Hollow had some life that represented normality, at one end of Goldsmith Way. That's how it was. People came and the lucky ones went. His community would never leave. He was gathering more and more. The complexities of every new age brought with it anguish, oppressive behaviour and aggression. It was torture for Lee Ping to watch the destruction of the human race.

He watched the blow-ins come and go. The Born and Bred watched from behind their lace curtains. Lee Ping's community watched their descendants with shame more often than pride. That's how it was in Ravens Hollow; the Sentinels worked assiduously to protect and serve. So many messages went unread.

Elva watched as her descendants multiplied, some good, some bad, never getting rid of the traits the preacher had passed on, like a reward they had earned.

Raylene cried and asked, 'Why do I have to see Jim Hartnell's nature being recreated time and time again?'

The Hartnell and Smiths' blood wound its way through the Hollow's veins like a red serpent spreading its poison.

Raylene could never escape Morrie's need for her love, love that she was never going to give. Raylene asked, 'Why, why, why?' She waited for an answer that would never come.

Brendan was still looking for his God and cursing his mother. He would never know peace. He watched Theo's offspring diminish, with sadness.

Fairy would watch every new owner of the Golden Nugget fight to make a profit, fight to keep the peace. She would never understand why Morrie had killed her when she had been so kind without judgement.

Tom Barlow watched with pride as the Barlow men protected everyone that passed through the Hollow. Lee Ping's descendants were the backbone that saved Ravens Hollow from the evil depravity rampant in this toxic town. Tom would stand tall beside Lee Ping forever.

Betty would roam, spreading her messages, with good intent, not to frighten but to save. No one ever listened. Her greatest joy was when Marion felt at peace; she heard her words even though she never understood. No one would ever understand the pain she experienced when she knew she was so wise (boondyil) (kulng ga long) (koo-chel) with the wisdom of the dancing ghost.

Roberta and Claudia watched as Jenny's Daughter came to Ravens Hollow. They watched as they saw her heading into a disastrous marriage to a Smith. It saddened them to see her leave, though they were relieved Angie and the child would be safe from the horror and afflictions that would have been placed on her if she had stayed.

Lee Ping watched as Jessica slowly went mad, talking to the noises coming from under the tree where the roots reached the bottom of Mabel Burns burial well.

The community of lost souls would drift and gather. The sentinels would do their job, with no reward. Life would change, life would stay the same.

Edwina Kelly-Price cried for Marion the night the glow of her soul left her body. She would never know that Marion's indigenous blood ran through the veins of her and her girls.

Sophie's daughter returned to the Mackenzie building many years later and the incestuous cycle would continue. Ravens Hollow on the inevitable path of destruction.

The miners, gold diggers, ripped away the land's true intent. Scarring never to be healed. Lee Ping would cry for his beloved China, for his first family, for Ravens Hollow, the assassination of the land of which he had been a part, the greed of man. Lee Ping would cry though sightless eyes for an eternity.

The End

Shawline Publishing Group Pty Ltd
www.shawlinepublishing.com.au

More great Shawline titles can be found here:

New titles also available through Books@Home Pty Ltd.
Subscribe today - www.booksathome.com.au